D0724840

THE LAST DAYS OF ADAM POWERS . . .

They would be anything but pleasant. He was saved from a hanging in Crow City, but he had only exchanged one death for another and he'd got the worst of the trade.

For Mike Hale was a cruel man who could think of a number of ways to kill an enemy slowly that would make an Apache appear tenderhearted.

Hale was serious. Dead serious. "I could let you go into town where they'd hang you, but that would be over in a few minutes. I've told myself a hundred times that if I ever got my hands on one of you bastards who killed Lon and Bud, I'd kill you slow and with all the misery I could think of. It ain't gonna be right off, though. I aim to let you think on it for a spell."

REVENGE
AT
CROW CITY

Wayne D. Overholser

REVENGE AT CROW CITY
A Bantam Book | April 1980

ISBN 0–553–13771–9

Published simultaneously in the United States and Canada

Bantam Books are published by Bantam Books, Inc. Its trademark, consisting of the words "Bantam Books" and the por-
trayal of a bantam, is Registered in U.S. Patent and Trademark
Office and in other countries. Marca Registrada. Bantam
Books, Inc., 666 Fifth Avenue, New York, New York 10019.

REVENGE
AT
CROW CITY

Chapter 1

As Sam Powers left the AP ranch house after dinner, he saw Sheriff Ed Garber turn off the county road and ride up the lane. He had no idea what the lawman wanted, but Sam was vaguely uneasy, because Garber represented settler law in Bensen County. That was just as far removed from justice on one side as big rancher law had been on the other side, in the days before the invasion.

Sam continued on to the corral and stopped beside the gate to wait for Garber. He rolled a smoke and fired it, wishing he was wearing his gun. He seldom wore it, because it was an invitation to trouble, particularly with feeling running as high as it had been ever since the invaders had been released from jail in Cheyenne. Sam's father, Adam Powers, had been a member of the invading party, so despite the fact that Sam had had no sympathy for the invaders, he had been tarred by the same brush in the eyes of the public.

A few minutes later Garber reached the house, saw Sam, and rode toward him, calling, "Howdy, Sam."

"Howdy, Ed," Sam said, nodding.

Garber reined up and leaned forward. "I suppose you've heard about Adam?"

Sam shook his head. "We haven't heard from Pa for quite a while. All we know is that he was turned loose with the rest of them and he'll be on his way home pretty soon."

"That's why I rode out," Garber said. "I just got a telegram from Casper. There's been a storm and the wires were down for a while, so the telegram was late

1

getting to me. Anyhow, he's coming in on the afternoon stage."

Sam hesitated, knowing there was more to Garber's visit than there appeared to be. It just wasn't in Ed Garber's makeup to ride out here from Crow City to tell him that Adam was arriving in town this afternoon.

"Thanks for bringing the word," Sam said. "Ma's been worried. She'll be glad to hear."

Garber cleared his throat. "There's something else, Sam. I don't want Adam to get to town. You know how folks are feeling. Or maybe you don't, being Adam's son. I guess you ain't been in town much lately."

"I ain't, for a fact," Sam said.

"Then I'll tell you," Garber said bluntly. "Folks figured for sure that the invaders would get their necks stretched for murder or at least go to the pen for life. Now that the whole kit and kaboodle of 'em has been let go scot free, folks are sore. I figure that if Adam shows up in town, there'll be a necktie party in his honor."

"You were elected to stop lynching, along with some other things that have been going on," Sam said.

"I'm one man," Garber said defensively. "The only deputy I've got is fifty miles away down on the Stinking Water looking into some horse stealing. I can't hold off a lynch mob, so I want you to meet the stage before it gets to town and take Adam off. See that he goes home and there won't be no trouble."

So that was it. Ed Garber wanted to prevent an explosive situation from developing more to save his hide than Adam Powers'. Sam shook his head. "It's up to you to keep the peace, Ed. I wouldn't do what you're asking even if it would work, which it won't. Pa is a proud man. He's likewise stubborn. I couldn't get him off that stage no matter what I did or said. He's never listened to me and he won't now. He'll ride the stage into Crow City come hell or high water."

"Damn it," Garber said, his face turning red, "you

can explain it to him, can't you? I ain't fixing to argue the right or the wrong of the invasion, or of Adam coming back, and I ain't gonna argue about the justice of 'em getting off like they done. All I want is to save some lives. I promise you that if Adam gets to town, there'll be some powder burned or a rope stretched or both."

"You don't know Pa like I do," Sam said. "I tell you he's mule stubborn. There's nothing I can do except to be in town when the stage gets there."

Garber chewed on his lower lip a moment, staring sullenly at Sam. Then he burst out, "You know and I know that if Adam Powers had had his way, he'd have strung me up when them bastards got to Crow City, along with just about every man in town. Folks in the county knows that, so what do you think is gonna happen when somebody that they think ought to hang for murder steps down from that stage a free man?"

"I'll be there," Sam said, "and I'll fetch Bronc Collins. If a mob tries anything, some of them will get killed. I don't think they're going to ask for that."

Garber didn't move for a full minute. He kept staring at Sam as if he couldn't believe what he'd heard; then suddenly he wheeled his horse, shouting, "I won't be there. I'm going fishing." He put his horse into a gallop and didn't look back.

Sam sucked in a long breath, thinking that this was a day he had hoped would never come. He looked around at the ranch buildings and the maze of corrals, remembering when the AP had been the biggest outfit in the county, when there had been a dozen cowhands riding for his dad and thousands of cattle carrying the AP brand.

Now the crew consisted of Sam and Bronc Collins, and there were hundreds of cattle instead of thousands. This had happened because the homesteaders had moved in by the scores and whittled the AP range down until nothing was left except the deeded land along the North Fork of Crow Creek and the summer range in the Big Horns.

"The damn sodbusters moved in on us like a plague of locusts," Adam had said before he'd left to join the invaders. "What do you do with locusts? You kill as many as you can, and by God, that's what I aim to do."

"That's murder," Sam had shouted at him. "You have no legal right to—"

"Then let it be murder," Adam had shouted back, "and to hell with what you call legal right. The cure has got to be big enough and tough enough to lick the disease."

That was the start of the quarrel and it had gone on from there. Sam had long been convinced that Adam was not capable of loving any human being except his wife, Ida, and sometimes Adam had not even shown that love as clearly as he should have. To the old man Sam was just another good cowhand who was made foreman when he grew up and continued as foreman as long as there was a need for one. He'd been too young for the job, but he had grown up when he was still a boy. Adam had seen to that.

Sam had never really quarreled with Adam before. He had understood as soon as he was big enough to understand anything that Adam's word was law and was not to be questioned. The one quarrel had been bitter, bitter enough to make Sam move out. The situation that brought it about had started nearly two years before, when Adam, in Cheyenne on business, heard for the first time the talk about a plan to raise a band of armed ranchers and gunmen, invade Bensen County, and hang every man who was a known rustler or horse thief.

For years Adam had been irrational when he talked about the settlers who had homesteaded on AP range, how they ate his beef and made a poor man out of him. In his eyes every settler in the county was a rustler, so the scheme fitted right into his thinking. He wouldn't have stopped with the list of known rustlers; he would have cleaned the range of homesteaders and restored the grass to stockmen.

He came home from Cheyenne and talked about it as if the old days would be restored after the hangings. Sam held his tongue until Adam received word the next spring that he was to be in Casper May first to join the invaders. That was when the quarrel erupted; Sam couldn't keep still any longer.

He told Adam that he would be as bad a lawbreaker as the rustlers and horse thieves, that he would make an outlaw out of himself, that the scheme was doomed to failure before it started. Adam insisted that the powerful men in the state, clear up to the governor, were on the side of the cattlemen and they couldn't lose. Or, if they did lose, the governor would see to it that they didn't come to trial.

In the end Adam lost his temper and accused Sam of siding with the settlers. He said he would no longer claim Sam as his son, so Sam had no choice but to pack up and move out. Mrs. Powers' tears had never changed Adam's mind in the past, and they didn't then.

After Adam left, Mrs. Powers persuaded Sam to come back to the AP, saying that Adam had said things he didn't mean and was sorry he had said them. Sam didn't believe that, but when his mother said she needed him, he couldn't refuse.

Sam, of course, had no idea how long Adam would be gone, or if he would ever return. The invasion failed, as Sam had known it would. Adam was arrested, along with the rest of the invaders, and held for a time in a nearby army post, because Bensen County had insufficient facilities to take care of that large a party of lawbreakers. In the end they were sent to Cheyenne. Now they had been released because Bensen County was broke and could not afford to prosecute. Adam had been right about one thing. The invaders were not brought to trial.

The incident was not ending as Sam and everyone else in Bensen County had thought it would. Adam was the one member of the invading party who lived near Crow City and who was personally known to everyone there. From the ugly talk Sam had heard, he was sure that the sheriff was right about what would happen when Adam stepped down from the stage; but regardless of the right or wrong of Adam's past actions, Sam had to do what he could to prevent his father's blood from being shed on the streets of Crow City.

He glanced at the sun and knew it was time to start. He wanted to reach Crow City ahead of the stage. The townsmen respected him enough to believe him, and he was reasonably sure that once he made it clear that he'd kill the first man who laid a hand on Adam, there would be no trouble. He shook his head and grimaced. He was fooling himself, and he was not a man who could do that for more than a few seconds.

He found Bronc Collins working on a fence north of the barn. He said, "Garber was just here. He told me that Adam is coming in on the stage. You hook up the buckboard. I'll tell Ma, then I'll saddle up and catch you."

Bronc tossed his hammer into the bucket of staples. "You figger on trouble?"

"There'll be plenty of trouble if I can't talk them out of it," Sam answered. "Put your gun on. It'll be you and me against the town. Garber made it clear he was going fishing."

"Sounds like that bastard," Bronc grunted.

"I don't figure on doing any shooting unless we're forced into it," Sam said, "but you know how they feel about Pa in town."

Bronc nodded. "They've hated him for years. Now it's a hell of a lot worse." He hesitated, eyeing Sam as he tugged at one end of his mustache. "Adam ain't one to forget and forgive, Sam. He'll kick you off the place again just like he done before."

"I figure as much," Sam said.

Bronc shrugged. "Well, I've come a long ways with that old bull. I might as well go the rest of the way."

Sam turned and strode toward the house. He hated to tell his mother. He had a feeling that the year Adam had been gone was the happiest year she'd had since she'd been married.

6

Chapter 2

Sam found his mother kneading bread on the kitchen table. She turned her head to see who had come in, smiled, and asked, "What brings you back into the house?"

"I've got something to tell you," he said. He crossed the room to the table and sat down.

Ida Powers was thirty years younger than Adam. She had married him when she was sixteen, more to escape her poverty-stricken home than because she loved him. Through the years she had learned how to live with him, seldom if ever opposing him, although there had been times when she had slowly and slyly diverted him from some of his ruthless plans without Adam suspecting what she was doing.

She was white-haired and plump, but she was still only forty, a fine-looking woman. Adam had always been proud of her. She had worked hard when they were first married, but after Adam had become wealthy, he had hired a woman to do the housework. As long as the AP crew had been a big one, there had always been a cook, and the men had eaten in the cookshack and stayed in the bunkhouse.

For the last few years, when Sam and Bronc Collins had made up the crew, Ida had done the cooking. Both men had lived in the main house after Adam had left. Ida had appreciated this, saying she was glad she didn't have to live in the big house by herself.

Now that Adam was returning, Sam had a feeling that he and Bronc would go back to the bunkhouse, if Adam didn't send him packing again. He rolled a smoke, thinking again of his job. If he could, he would stay for his mother's sake, he told himself. He would know his future when he heard the first words that Adam spoke when he stepped off the stage in Crow City.

Sam didn't speak for a time, not wanting to say anything, but knowing he had to. He couldn't be sure how his mother would feel about Adam's return, but he had a feeling that if she had her druthers, Adam would stay away forever. After devoting twenty-four years of her life to a man who had never shown very much appreciation for that devotion, it was only natural that she would enjoy a year of freedom and feel she would like to have that year go on and on.

"Well?" Ida asked, looking directly at him. "You don't seem very anxious to give me the news."

"I'm not," Sam said, "but here goes. Garber was out right after dinner. He told me that Adam was coming in on the afternoon stage."

Her face froze and turned white. She sat down abruptly, her eyes fixed on Sam. "I . . . I knew he would be home sometime," she said in a low tone. "I guess I just didn't think it would be this soon. Well, I'll have to clean house."

"Let it go," Sam said. "Why don't you tell Pa that from now on, the house is your ballywick?"

She smiled faintly. "Sam, you always said that nobody tells Adam anything. No, it's easier to clean house." She wiped her face with her handkerchief. "What will you do, Sam? I can't face you leaving home again."

"Even to marry Betty?"

She nodded. "Even to marry Betty. I know that isn't going to happen right away, but Adam will be here in a few hours."

"You're right about me not marrying Betty right away," he said morosely. "Not with her pa on the warpath every day the way he is. But I don't know about Adam. Bronc and me are meeting the stage, and we'll get him home alive if we can. I suppose I'll stay if he lets me."

She nodded. "He knows you've been here ever since

he left, but he's never mentioned it in his letters. I think he expected you to come back and live here, and I also think he'll want you to stay. He just won't say so."

Sam nodded agreement. "It's my guess he'll act as if nothing happened before he left. Garber wanted me to take him off the stage before it got to town, but I told him I couldn't do that. Pa wouldn't get off that stage for anything or anybody before it pulls up in front of the hotel."

"That's right, he wouldn't," she agreed. "He'll have it out with the town first thing. He was never one to put anything off." She sighed. "I wonder if he's changed."

"You think he could?"

"Yes, I do," Ida said. "I've sensed it in his letters. A year in jail facing hanging or a life term in prison would change anybody." She shrugged. "I don't know, Sam. It would help if he could just face life in Bensen County like it is and not the way it was ten years ago. I guess no one likes change, but Adam has had a crazy kind of sickness to go on pretending that everything was the way it used to be."

That was true, but it surprised him to hear her say it. He rose. "I'd better get moving. I'll do the best I can for him, Ma."

"I know you will." She rose and, as he came around the table, she put her arms around him. "But don't get killed on his account. He's an old man and he's had a full life. You're young and your life should be just starting."

"I don't aim to get killed," Sam said.

She turned away and started to cry. He strode out of the house, thinking it was the first time she had hugged him since he'd been a boy. He had known she loved him, but she had never been one to show it. Adam had always laughed at people who showed feelings of any kind. He said they were soft, so Ida had learned to hide her feelings.

Sam saddled up and took the road to Crow City. Two miles from town he turned south and rode past the Rock Creek school, where Betty Arbanz taught.

Another quarter of a mile brought him to the Arbanz place. He reined up in front of the house and sat motionless for a time.

He had never understood why Tony Arbanz, who had moved here from Cheyenne two years ago and bought the Crow City *Sentinel,* had chosen to live out here instead of in town. Sam figured it was because Tony had taken the homesteaders' side from the moment he had moved to Bensen County, and he thought he'd better live in the country the way they did.

Tony had bought a choice quarter section and built a house. It was his home and he saw no reason to change or move. Besides, it was close enough for Betty to walk to school. During the winter months when the weather was cold, Tony said it was easier for him to buck the snowdrifts and wind for two and a half miles than it would be for Betty to ride out from town.

Sam did not understand Tony, who was a complicated man and in many ways a strange one. Sam wasn't even sure he was completely sane. He thrived on hate for all big cattlemen and everyone and everything connected with them. He had nothing against Sam personally, but Sam was connected to the AP, which had been one of the big outfits; therefore, he hated Sam. Irrational, but Tony Arbanz was that way. Everything was black or white. He had forbidden Sam to see Betty, promising to shoot him if he ever showed up at the Arbanz house.

Arbanz had used his editorials in the *Sentinel* to warn Adam not to return to Bensen County, saying that he'd face a hangman's knot if he did. Now that Adam was disregarding the warning, Arbanz was capable of organizing a lynch party.

Sam paused for a full minute before he dismounted, thinking that if Arbanz was home, he would soon know it. Months ago Betty and Sam had agreed on a signal. She would always have a dishcloth on the line when it was safe for him to stop. There was no dishcloth on the line now, so he was breaking his agreement with her.

Suddenly Sam wished he hadn't stopped. If Arbanz did shoot him, he didn't want it to happen in the man's front yard with Betty watching. He reined his horse around and started to ride away, deciding he was taking a stupid risk by staying, when Betty ran out of the house, calling, "Sam! Wait, Sam."

He turned his horse and reined up. A moment later he was on the ground and she was in his arms, hugging and kissing him, and trembling with fear. Finally she was able to say, "Daddy just left here. He must have cut across the Hempstead place or you'd have run into him. When I looked out and saw you, I was too scared to move. I was afraid he was close enough to see you."

"This is gonna stop," Sam said. "If you marry me, he'll have to accept me as a son-in-law. The way it is now, he thinks he can shoot me and live with his conscience, but if we were married, he wouldn't shoot your husband."

"I've come to the same conclusion," she said. "I know it's got to stop. It's not as if we were doing anything wrong. It's just his unreasonable, stupid hate." She tipped her head back and smiled. "But is Adam any different?"

"No, he's crazy, too," Sam admitted. "Right now, with the invaders turned loose and folks feeling the way they do, I'm not sure how many other people in the county are just as kill crazy."

"Daddy says lots of them agree with him," she said. "You've heard that Adam is coming in on the stage?"

He nodded. "That's why I stopped by. I thought you might not have heard. I'm headed for town now. I'll try to get Pa out of town alive. I thought you ought to know about it. Something could happen to me or Tony before it's over."

"Daddy told me," she said. "That's why he came home this afternoon. He said what you just said, that this whole thing is coming to a head. I think he knows that we've been seeing each other, but he just kind of hinted. All he said was for me to keep you out of town this afternoon. He doesn't want me to marry you, but he doesn't want you hurt, either."

"He aims to lynch Pa?"

11

"I think so," she said. "He didn't say it in so many words, but he gave me that impression." She turned and walked away, frowning thoughtfully, then came back. "Sam, I hadn't really given much thought to it, but it didn't make sense for him to tell me that. I'm sure that he does know we've been seeing each other, so he's just been ignoring it."

"I suppose he cleared his conscience by acting like he didn't know," Sam said. "Anyhow, I think you're right. It would be easier for him and his bunch if I wasn't in town, so he figured he could use you to keep me out."

"He doesn't know you very well." She smiled and shook her head. "You're just as stubborn as he is. Or Adam. I won't even ask you not to go into town."

"Good." He put his arms around her again. "Listen. I don't know what Adam will say when he gets home, but I don't aim to stay if he says he doesn't want me. We'll get married and leave. I don't know what we'll do or where we'll go, but we'll get along."

"Of course we will," she said. "I'll write my letter of resignation this afternoon." She hesitated, then asked, "But what if Adam wants you to stay?"

"You can live with Ida," he said. "She told me she'd love to have you."

"No, Sam," she said. "It wouldn't work."

"Well then, we'll build a little house beside the big one," he said. "Or work the bunkhouse over." He kissed her and stepped into the saddle. "Either way we'll get married."

"That's right," she said. "Anything is better than the way we've been living. I want it all out in the open."

He rode away, not looking back. He was glad the situation was coming to a head. He agreed with Betty that anything was better than the way they had been living. Then a shocking question came to him. What would happen if he killed Tony this afternoon?

Betty had much the same feeling for her father that he had about Adam, both loving and hating him. Tony Arbanz had always been a possessive, smothering father who tried to make her decisions for her. She would probably be relieved if he were dead, but by Sam Powers' hand? No, he told himself bitterly. It just wouldn't do, but it could happen.

Chapter 3

Adam Powers leaned against the back of the stage-coach seat, his gaze on the good-looking young woman who rode facing him. Only three passengers were on the stage: Adam, the young woman, and a drummer who was headed for Crow City and on north to Sheridan. All of them had boarded the stage at Casper. Several ranchers' wives had started with them, but had gotten off farther south, so only the three remained. Now that they had nearly reached the end of the long, tedious journey, Adam knew no more about the woman than he had when they had left Casper.

He glanced out the window and saw that they had almost reached the top of Crow Hill. From then on, it would be downgrade all the way to Crow City. In just a few minutes he would be facing a hostile town. No one had told him that or written it to him, but he knew it would be that way. Some things people forgot, but the Crow City folks and the homesteaders who lived in Bensen County would never forget that he, Adam Powers, had been one of the leaders of the invaders.

He didn't know how far they'd go when he stepped down from the coach. Well, by God, he'd spit in their eyes. Maybe they'd just curse him. They might tar and feather him. That would be something Tony Arbanz would think of. Or they might have a hanging

13

rope wating for him, a rope they had expected the county to give him legally. He had failed, he thought bitterly, his friends had failed, and the invasion had accomplished nothing beyond the killing of Lon Hale and Bud Larkin. It was those killings for which the Bensen County people thought he and the other invaders should have been hanged.

He had no regrets about the two killings. Hale and Larkin were known rustlers; they had been on the list of marked men, and they had deserved killing. But he did regret the time wasted on them, time they had kept the invading party from pushing on and catching the Crow City people unprepared.

Damn it, if the raiders had only moved faster, if they had bypassed Hale and Larkin, they could have nailed at least twenty of the rustler bunch in town, then fanned out through the countryside and wiped the rustlers out for good.

Too much bickering among the leaders. They had refused to listen to him. He was still angry about that. He knew this country, he knew the people, and he should have been given command. But no, the job had gone to Colonel Seth Alexander, who was a political power in the state and probably the richest cattleman.

If any one man could be blamed for the failure, it was Alexander. He'd had a personal feud with Lon Hale. Alexander's ranch was on the North Platte. Lon Hale and his brother Mike had lived in the area and had stolen cattle from him. Alexander had succeeded in chasing them out of that part of the country, but hadn't caught up with them. They had moved north and settled in Bensen County. Lon and his friend Bud Larkin in the southern end of the county, and Mike a few miles southeast of the AP.

Alexander wasn't going to miss this chance to kill Lon Hale, so the party had been held up nearly twenty-four hours before Hale and his partner had been rooted out of their cabin and shot to death. Alexander had been disappointed that the second man was Bud Larkin and not Mike Hale, but even if it had been

Mike, they were still small fry and not worth the time they cost.

The big ones were in Crow City. The sheriff. Tony Arbanz. The banker, Jason Small. The storekeeper, Fred Ames. And others. Men of that caliber were the ones who had made wholesale rustling possible in Bensen County. The sheriff winked at rustling. Small's bank loaned money to the rustlers when they needed it. Ames gave them credit at the store. Tony Arbanz was a firebrand who kept everybody in the county stirred up with his lurid stories of what would happen when the invaders reached Crow City.

It was water over the dam now, he told himself bitterly. If he lived long enough to get out of Crow City, he would go home to a ranch that was no longer a ranch. Land that he owned, sure, but there were only a few acres left that homesteaders had not moved onto. The situation was the same as when he'd left. Every cow thief in the county still had a license to steal.

Adam was going home to a wife who probably wished he had stayed in Cheyenne. He had always loved her, but she had borne him only one son and he wanted more. Maybe it wasn't her fault, but damn it, other women had given their husbands a dozen sons.

Then his thoughts turned to the one son Ida had given him. He was proud of Sam, a chip off the old block. Stupid, maybe, not able to see which side his bread was buttered on. Too easygoing. Not tough enough for this country, but by God, he had guts, enough guts to defy Adam, enough to get on a horse and ride off the AP, all the time knowing he would be disinherited.

Maybe Sam was tougher than Adam had realized. Suddenly and unexpectedly, he felt a compelling desire to see both of them again, Sam and Ida, to feel a horse between his legs, to ride out across his grass, or what was left of it, to see once more a steer carrying the AP iron.

He wondered if Sam would be in Crow City when the stage pulled in. He knew from Ida's letters that the boy had returned to the AP, that he and old Bronc had kept the place up, but he wasn't sure whether Sam would stay once Adam was back. He wouldn't urge Sam, he told himself. Sam would do what he damned pleased, and he'd better stay out of whatever trouble waited for Adam in town. He always had stomped his own snakes and he could do it now.

He turned his gaze again to the woman who sat across from him. Black hair, brown eyes almost as dark as her hair, eyes that sparkled with spirit. He had made an effort to talk to her, but she had wanted no part of it. He and the drummer had alternated seats so neither had had to ride backwards all the way, thus permitting the woman to keep the same seat. She had offered to take her turn riding backwards, but the men had not allowed it. The drummer had carried on a conversation with her, but all Adam could get out of her was a yes, a no, or a grunt.

Maybe she was a whore hoping to lure the drummer into bed with her once they reached Crow City. She was dressed well, with a broad-brimmed gray hat and a purple plume that seemed too long to Adam. She wore a linen duster, and although he had not seen much of the dress under the duster, he judged that it was silk.

In the early days there had been a brothel in Crow City, but the homesteader element had shut it down, once they had elected their own sheriff. He shrugged his shoulders. It made no never mind to him. He wasn't any good in bed any more. The last year as a prisoner had made an old man out of him.

He leaned his head against the back of the seat and closed his eyes. He was tired. Damn it, he had been tired ever since the invasion had failed and the invaders had been taken prisoner. He realized he'd be dead if the army hadn't interfered. The homesteaders had swarmed in like angry bees and had surrounded the raiding party on the Flying W twenty miles south of Crow City. They had every intention of wiping the invaders out to a man, and they would have if the army hadn't showed up. Still, he often thought he'd be as well off dead as to be the worn-out hull of a man he had become.

The coach groaned and creaked as it climbed the last steep pitch of the Crow Hill grade before it reached the summit. Adam was jarred from his somber thoughts by a yell. "Pull up, driver. Right there. Don't make a wrong move or it will be your last."

Startled, Adam looked through a window to see three men, their faces covered by bandannas, standing at the edge of the road, rifles lined on the stage driver. One man was squat and short-bodied, one was tall and lanky, and the third was a slender kid who had the awkward appearance of having just sprouted up out of his cowhide boots. Adam didn't recognize any of them, although he sensed a familiar quality in the voice of the squat man.

"I ain't carrying no strongbox," the driver said. "You're wasting your time holding us up."

"I reckon not," the squat man said. "You've got somebody inside we want."

Adam glanced at the woman, who had turned pale. She sat motionless, her fingers clutching her handbag so tightly that they were white. The drummer was sweating as he looked at the woman, then at Adam, and said in a low voice, "They don't want me. Nobody knows I'm on this stage."

It must be the woman, Adam thought. Then the door opened and the squat man poked his gun barrel into the coach. "Out, old man," he said to Adam. "Out."

Adam swallowed and shook his head, telling himself this couldn't be happening. It must be a nightmare. Nobody wanted him except the people who were waiting for him in Crow City. He said, "You ain't taking me nowhere, mister. I'm going to Crow City."

"I'm taking you, all right," the squat man said. "Now

17

me'n my friend here can go in after you and pry you out if we have to, but there's a lady inside and we don't want to worry her. It'll be a messy business if we have to do that. Or you can get out peaceful-like and there won't be no trouble."

The woman was staring at him as if she hoped he wouldn't make a fight out of it. The drummer was wiping his face with a handkerchief as he said with relief, "Better do what he says."

"All right," Adam said. "We don't want to worry the lady, do we?"

He had no idea why they wanted him, but the possibility that they were saving him from a hanging in Crow City did occur to him. He dismissed the thought at once. He didn't have a guess as to who they were, and he couldn't think of anyone except Sam or Bronc Collins who would even want to save him.

He stepped down from the coach, and the squat man slammed the door shut as he yelled, "Roll it, driver."

The squat man stepped back, his rifle covering Adam. The lanky man stood beside him. The kid kept his Winchester on the driver until the coach had moved up the grade; then he lowered the rifle and turned toward a steep-walled gully beside the road. Four horses were tied there.

The squat man motioned to Adam. "Slide down, old man. You'll get your pants dirty, but there's worse things than that."

"I ain't going anywhere till you tell me what you want with me," Adam said.

"Oh, you're going, all right," the squat man said grimly, "but then, I don't mind telling you what I want you for. I could let you go into town, where they'd hang you, but that would be over in a few minutes. I've told myself a hundred times that if I ever got my hands on one of you bastards who murdered Lon and Bud, I'd kill you slow and with all the misery I could think of. It ain't gonna be right off, though. I aim to let you think on it for a spell."

18

Adam knew, then, even before the squat man jerked off his bandanna. He was Mike Hale, the older brother of Lon Hale, who had been killed by the invaders. He should have recognized Hale's voice. He'd heard it often enough in Crow City the year before the invasion. Hale was a bully, a carouser, a wicked barroom brawler, a rustler, and a troublemaker. He was, in Adam's opinion, the worst of a bad lot.

Unexpectedly, Adam laughed. He'd had a fleeting hope that he was being saved from a hanging in Crow City, but he had only exchanged one death for another, and he'd got the worst of the trade. Mike Hale was a cruel man who could think of a number of ways to kill an enemy slowly that would make an Apache appear tenderhearted.

"Laugh, you old goat," Hale said, suddenly furious. "It'll be the last laugh you have for a while."

He gave Adam a shove that sent him sprawling over the edge of the gully. He rolled down the steep, rock-strewn slope, to land in the sand at the bottom, dust rising around him. The others had already reached the horses. When Adam, the wind knocked out of him, failed to get up, Hale yanked him to his feet.

"You ain't hurt," Hale said. "Get aboard." He motioned to a short-legged bay. "Watch him, Marty. He's a tricky old cuss. I don't want to lose him now."

Hale wheeled, mounted, and rode up the gully to the top of Crow Hill and disappeared over the crest. The lanky man and the kid had already mounted. Both had removed their bandannas, but Adam didn't recognize either one.

Adam painfully pulled himself into the saddle, thinking that he'd be riding across the grass, all right, but it wouldn't be his grass and he wouldn't be seeing Ida or Sam. He wouldn't see any AP steers, either. He wouldn't be seeing much of anything from now on.

Chapter 4

Sam caught up with Bronc Collins and the buckboard a quarter of a mile out of Crow City, just before the east–west county road joined the north–south road that became the town's main street and ran on to Sheridan.

Sam saw that Bronc's Winchester leaned against the seat beside him. He studied the old man's face as they made the turn toward town, but Bronc's face was grim and hard set, and Sam couldn't tell anything about what he was thinking.

The thought crossed Sam's mind, as it had a number of times, that maybe Adam Powers wasn't worth saving, at least not at the cost of the lives of other men who had had nothing to do with the invasion. But the thought didn't linger. You couldn't, he told himself, decide your actions on that basis. What Arbanz and his bunch planned to do was just as wrong as what Adam Powers and his fellow invaders had done.

A few minutes later they were in town. They passed a scattering of houses, mostly log cabins, then drove through one block of fine, two-story dwellings, several of them made of brick. This section was referred to by the homesteaders as Prosperity Row. The rich and powerful lived here, men who would have been lynched if the invaders had succeeded in their plan: Fred Ames, Jason Small, and others of their social and financial position. They would do the actual hanging today, Sam told himself bitterly, while the homesteaders gave them moral support, and no court in Bensen County would punish them.

They crossed the bridge that spanned Crow Creek

20

and rode into the business part of town. Sam was surprised at the size of the crowd. Horses and rigs of various kinds lined both sides of Main Street. Groups of men, mostly homesteaders, were scattered along the board walks, but there was not a single woman or child, a fact that added to the dark sense of foreboding that gripped Sam. He didn't see any guns, but a mob of this size didn't need guns. Sheer numbers would be enough.

Sam had hoped to stop in front of the hotel so he could move Adam from the stage to the buckboard in a matter of seconds, but there was no room. He nodded at Bronc, who glanced questioningly at him, and they rode on down the street until they found a vacant spot at the north end of the block. Sam dismounted and tied as Bronc swung the team toward the hitch rack, stepped down, and tied. He returned to the buckboard, picked up his Winchester, and joined Sam on the walk.

Sam had heard nothing from the crowd as he had ridden through town. The men were still standing silent and motionless as they stared at him and Bronc. Probably all of them recognized him, although he knew only a few of them. They also would know why he and Bronc were here. Now, as the two AP men strode toward the hotel, no one in the crowd tried to bar their way, but there was no mistaking the feeling of hostility that the homesteaders and townsmen felt. It was as intangible as smoke, but just as real.

When Sam reached the front of the hotel, he saw that Arbanz, Small, and Ames were standing directly across the street in front of the *Sentinel* office. They were staring at him, as if trying to determine his feeling and intent. He hesitated a moment, then decided it would be good strategy to put any doubts to rest.

"Stay here," he told Bronc, and crossed the street to stand directly in front of Arbanz.

For a moment their eyes met, but Sam had no intention of staring the man down. He turned to Ames, a burly man who resembled a blacksmith more than a storekeeper, who stood on one side of Arbanz. Then

21

he swung his gaze to Small, who stood on the other side of the *Sentinel* editor. The banker was a graying wisp of a man who looked as if a breeze would blow him over, but Sam knew how deceiving his appearance was. Jason Small was all steel. If Tony Arbanz ever faltered, Small was right there to goad him on.

Small's eyes were hard and defiant. He said, "I'm sorry you're here, Sam. It will not be pleasant for you."

Sam hesitated, wondering to what extent Small was the guiding hand behind this. There was no way to know. He turned to Arbanz and said, "Tony, you've put the word out. I reckon these men are here to watch the hanging."

"That's right," Arbanz said in his short, clipped way of speaking. "We aim to take your father as soon as he steps out of the stage, and we'll hang him from that big cottonwood just below the bridge. Remember, it's what he would have done to us if he had succeeded in doing what he and the others planned."

"I never agreed with what they planned and you know it," Sam said, "but what you're planning is murder just the same. I always thought a newspaper was supposed to be defending the law, not destroying it."

"That's right." Arbanz nodded. "I regret the necessity of taking the law into our hands, but what you must remember is that fifty men, because of their wealth and political power, are escaping scot free from any punishment for the murders they committed. That is not justice. When the law malfunctions, the citizens who live under that law must see that justice is performed."

There was no use to argue with that kind of logic, no use to point out where that reasoning would take a man if he followed it to its logical conclusion. It had been the same with Adam when he had announced he was leaving for Casper to join the invaders. There comes a time in the affairs of men when logic has no influence on those men's behavior. Sam had learned that with his father, and now he had a crazy feeling that he was treading the same path today.

Suddenly Sam was aware that Ames held a coiled rope in his hands. Arbanz reached out and took it from him. He lifted it waist high as he flipped the hangman's knot on one end back and forth. He said, "Don't make any trouble, Sam. There's too many of us."

"I came over here to tell you that I intend to make a hell of a lot of trouble for you if you lay a hand on Pa," Sam said. "I can see there's a lot of you, but before you do the job, Bronc and me will kill half a dozen of you. We'll get the ones in front. That'll be you, Tony. And Jason. And Fred."

He wheeled and strode back across the dust strip, not sure that he had accomplished anything, but at least he had given his warning. He and Bronc would probably die in the fracas. Or be tried and hanged for murder if they survived the fight.

"Well?" Bronc asked when Sam joined him. "What good did all that palaver do?"

"None," Sam said. "They're hell bent on hanging Pa."

"I could have told you that," Bronc said sourly.

For a time Sam and Bronc stood motionless, Sam keeping his eyes on the three men across the street. The homesteaders who had lined both sides of the business block began moving toward the hotel. It was not, Sam thought, due to any prearrangement. Rather, it was almost time for the stage, and they wanted to be on hand when Adam was taken from the coach. For a moment Sam had his doubts about how much he and Bronc could accomplish if the mob charged them; then he put the question out of his mind. He didn't believe that a mob of homesteaders would take any sharp or decisive action. They would be hesitant, he thought, and if that hesitation lasted more than a few seconds, Arbanz, Ames, and Small would be dead. When that happened, the chances were the mob would scatter.

John Doyle stepped out of the hotel and joined Sam. He said, "You shouldn't be here."

Doyle owned the hotel; he was the one man in Crow

City Sam felt was on his side. Doyle had come here in the early days, when the town was no more than a collection of log cabins and there were only a handful of ranches in the area. He had built the first hotel, a four-room log structure, then a few years later had put up the present two-story frame building.

The other early businessmen who had sympathized with the ranchers had left, but Doyle had hung on, partly because he liked the town and the surrounding country, and partly because his business had not been hurt by the influx of homesteaders. The people who stayed in the hotel were largely drummers, along with a few tourists who came for the hunting, and a few land seekers. The other businessmen in town left Doyle alone and he left them alone, and on that basis they got along.

Sam didn't say anything for a moment. Doyle was a big man, as big as Fred Ames. He had a small ranch in the foothills of the Big Horns that he used for a hunting lodge as much as anything. He was ruddy-faced and hard-muscled, and he bragged that he had never had a hunting partner who could outhike or outclimb him.

"Be damned queer if I was anywhere else, wouldn't it?" Sam asked finally.

"Knowing you and Bronc, I guess that's right," Doyle said, "but knowing Adam, I say he ain't worth it."

"I've had that thought," Sam admitted, "and I've been ashamed of it. Being an ornery, stubborn old goat doesn't keep him from being my pa."

"I reckon that's right," Doyle agreed, "but if you've got a notion of stopping 'em, you're crazy. There's too many of 'em."

"Tony just told me that," Sam said, "but I didn't believe him."

Doyle gave him a small grin. "No, you wouldn't." He scratched the back of his neck. "One thing, though, which I figure you don't know. These sodbusters all look calm enough. Easygoing. Like they wouldn't get worked up about anything. Well, that's wrong. I know 'em better'n you do and I've heard the talk long before the invasion and a hell of a lot since. Light a fuse and they're animals, Sam. Seeing Adam get off that stage is all the lighted fuse they'll need. Tony and his pals across the street know that and they're counting on it. Adam's blood won't be on their hands. You can depend on that."

Sam had told himself it wouldn't work that way, but he had to admit that Doyle knew the homesteaders better than he did. Suddenly someone yelled, "It's coming."

Doyle glanced at his watch. "Old Zeke's late today. Something must have slowed him up."

Sam was aware that the homesteaders were pushing forward toward the front of the hotel. He glanced around and saw that guns had appeared in their hands, mostly hand guns that had been carried under the waistbands of their pants. He felt a chill ravel down his spine. He glanced at Bronc, wondering if the old man was having a similar chill, but he still couldn't tell what the cowboy was thinking. Even in the early days, when Adam had been riding high and would chew Bronc out for something, he never showed even a hint of emotion.

Sam glanced over the crowd again, noting that it had flowed into the street between him and Arbanz and his friends. Doyle was right. Arbanz and the others wouldn't need to bloody their hands today. There was still no sound from the crowd, but to Sam the silence was more ominous than if they had been shouting. He felt a cold and deadly purpose in these bearded men. It must have been the same a year ago when word had reached them that the invaders had been surrounded on the Flying W.

He took a deep breath, the chill that ran down his spine almost paralyzing him. God, there were a lot of them. The number had grown ever since he and Bronc had arrived in town. The homesteaders had pressed forward to form a solid bank in the street and on both sides of Sam.

He turned to Doyle. "Which side are you on, John?"

"You ought to know," Doyle snapped. "I never got along with the plowpushers."

"We could use another gun," Sam said.

"The hell you could!" Doyle looked at him, outraged. "Do I look like a man who wants to commit suicide?"

"You sure don't," Sam said, "but we might have a chance with another gun. Maybe you're afraid to show which side you're on?"

Doyle glared at him a moment, then wheeled, stepped into the lobby, and returned with a long-barreled .45. He said harshly, "I'm as big an idiot as you are, Sam, and with less reason, but you're right about showing which side I'm on. If I live through the afternoon, I'll be able to sleep tonight."

The stage had reached the bottom of Crow Hill and was thundering toward the center of town, the horses on a dead run, the way Zeke Partridge always brought them in. They pounded across the bridge, hoofs cracking against the plank floor with staccato sharpness, then came on to the hotel, the homesteaders opening up so the stage had a path through them.

Zeke pulled up in front of the hotel in a cloud of dust not more than ten feet from Sam, who moved toward the coach, Bronc and Doyle a step behind him. Zeke had swung down and opened the door, calling as he always did, "End of the line. All out for Crow City."

The homesteaders were pressing against Sam, who now could see into the coach. Suddenly, in disbelief, he realized that his father was not there. Zeke helped a woman passenger down; then a drummer stepped out.

"I'll get your luggage and take it into the hotel for you," Zeke said.

He closed the door as a dozen voices bellowed, "Where's Adam Powers?"

Zeke held up a gnarled hand. "Sorry, boys. Adam

got off the stage on the other side of the summit of Crow Hill."

The crowd that had been pressing against Sam fell back, and a path opened for the woman passenger and the drummer. Doyle followed them into the lobby. Zeke pushed several homesteaders back as he worked his way around the coach to the rear boot.

Somebody asked, "Why did Powers get off the stage?"

"All I know, boys, is he didn't have no choice," Zeke said. "Three masked men with guns took him."

Chapter 5

The stage drove away and the homesteaders, tight-lipped and silent, slowly returned to their horses and rigs. Sam stood on the walk in front of the hotel, stunned, completely puzzled by what had happened. He could not understand it; he could not even guess who had taken his father off the stage or what the motive had been.

Tony Arbanz stood a few feet from Sam, staring at him with unadulterated hatred in his eyes. Sam had not felt that in the homesteaders. Rather, he sensed that they had been relieved that they had not had to face the grim responsibility of hanging a man. Sam doubted that Arbanz and his friends would ever get the mob together again for that purpose. Normally the homesteaders were hard-working, peace-loving settlers. Being part of a hanging mob was not natural for them.

Ames and Small had left, but apparently the malevolent spirit of revenge burned brighter in Arbanz

27

than the other two. Sam had never understood why the editor felt so strongly about Adam Powers, but he had expressed his attitude in the *Sentinel* often enough for the past year.

Sam turned toward the hotel door, saying to Bronc Collins, "Go on home, Bronc. I'll be along. If I'm not back in time for supper, tell Ma to keep it warm for me."

Bronc nodded and walked toward the buckboard. Arbanz asked, "How did you do it, Sam?"

"I didn't," Sam said. "I expected Pa to be on that stage as much as you did."

"Who did it for you?" Arbanz asked doggedly.

"Damn it, I told you I had nothing to do with it," Sam said, losing control of his temper. "I'm not going to tell you again. I don't know who did it and I don't know why."

"That's pretty slim." Arbanz shook his head in obvious disbelief. "The sheriff notified you that your father would be on the stage and asked you to take him off before he reached town. You knew that you and Collins would be the only men who'd defend your father. That's why you came to town, wasn't it?"

"That's right," Sam said, "but if I had hired someone to take Pa off the stage, I wouldn't have come to town."

"We're not done," Arbanz said. "I'll tell you one thing. We will never let your father live in this community again."

Sam started toward the hotel lobby, then stopped. He said, "I'll be in to see you in a day or so about something else, but this ain't the day."

"If it's about Betty, forget it," Arbanz said. "You'll never have her."

Sam went on into the hotel lobby, ignoring Arbanz's statement. He didn't really expect the editor to change his attitude, but at least he would let the man know what his alternatives were. Arbanz was a violent man, he was a man of set opinions, but he was also an intelligent man and he loved Betty, so Sam hoped some middle ground could be found.

Sam walked to the desk. Doyle was not in sight and no clerk was on duty at the moment. Sam turned the register and saw that the drummer's name was Rodney Blake and the woman was named Julie Larkin. If the holdup men were masked, as Zeke had said, the chance that either Blake or the Larkin woman could tell him anything was slim, but at least he could ask.

He glanced into the dining room. It was empty, so he crossed the lobby and stepped into the bar. Blake was sitting at a table with a bottle in front of him. Sam walked to his table and said, "I'm Sam Powers. I'd like to talk to you."

Blake rose and gave Sam a soft hand. "Sit down." He motioned to the chair across the table from him. "You related to the old man who was taken off the stage?"

"I'm his son," Sam said. "That's what I want to talk to you about."

"From what I saw after we got into town," Blake said, "it was a good thing for your father that he wasn't on the stage. I never saw a mob like this one. They didn't say anything, but they didn't need to. Those fellows meant business. You could feel it."

"What I want to know," Sam said, "is who took Pa off the stage. What did the men look like?"

"I don't know," Blake said. "Their faces were covered. The one who did the talking was short and heavy-set. He had the biggest shoulders I ever saw on a man." Blake laughed shortly. "But then I wasn't seeing anything the right size. I'd swear his gun was a cannon."

"You didn't see or hear anything that would give me a clue about who he was?"

Blake shook his head. "No sir, I didn't. I didn't see the other men. Not much of them anyhow. The one up in front who kept the driver covered wasn't in my view at all, but I glimpsed the second man. He was tall and pretty thin. Aside from that, he might have been any cowboy in the county."

"They didn't give you any notion about what they were going to do with Pa?"

"No," Blake said, then he frowned. "Well, he told your father to get out of the coach and your father said he wouldn't do it. Then the holdup man said he and his friend could pry him out of the coach, but that would worry the lady. Or he said you can get out peaceful-like and there wouldn't be any trouble, so your father got out." Blake shook his head. "But that's not much help, is it?"

"Not much." Sam rose. "Thank you, Mr. Blake." He started toward the door into the lobby, then stopped and turned back. "The woman's name is Julie Larkin. Who is she and why did she come to Crow City?"

"I can't tell you," Blake said. "She was mighty private. She didn't say anything that meant anything all the way from Casper. Your father tried to talk to her, but she wouldn't talk. I did a little better, but our conversation never got beyond the weather and the dust and how hard the seat was." He paused and scratched his head. "But she was scared. I don't think she had anything to do with the three men."

"Probably not," Sam agreed, and went into the lobby.

John Doyle was behind the desk. Sam paused, asking, "Have you talked to the woman who got off the stage?"

Doyle nodded, not meeting Sam's gaze. "She's upstairs in room 20. I reckon you'll want to talk to her, but I don't figure she can tell you anything."

"I'll find out," Sam said, and climbed the stairs, wondering why Doyle had suddenly become uneasy.

Room 20 was at the end of the hall, its window looking down on Main Street. Sam knocked, and the woman asked, "Who is it?"

"Sam Powers," he said.

She opened the door at once, saying, "Come in, Mr. Powers. I was hoping I'd have a chance to talk to you."

She closed the door behind him and pointed to a

straight-backed chair. She said, "Sit down, please. I was sitting in the rocker by the window. My brother used to write to me about how Crow City was a quiet little cowtown where nothing any more serious happened than having a horse act up and buck its rider off on Main Street."

She took her seat again in the rocking chair. Sam sat down, uneasy for some reason that he did not understand. He perched his hat on one knee and looked at the woman. She was in her early twenties, he judged, very attractive, and wearing a blue silk dress with a tight lace collar. It must, he told himself, be a very expensive dress and not the kind the women he knew wore. She didn't look like the average woman traveler who stepped down from the stage in Crow City.

She sat with her hands folded on her lap, demure and shy, and yet, paradoxically, bold. He'd had little to do with women except Betty Arbanz and his mother, and now, realizing that, he felt even more uneasy. He had a feeling this woman had been everywhere and had done everything. The boldness that he sensed did not come from anything she said or did, but rather was an intangible quality about her. It was real, he thought. The demure and shy appearance that she gave was not.

"I was frightened when those men took your father off the stage," she said. "They are vicious men. The one who did the talking said something about making trouble if he didn't get out of the stage. He said that might worry the lady, and of course your father got out then, saying he didn't want to do that. I think those men really want to kill your father, Mr. Powers. I don't think he's safe."

"Why didn't they let him come on to town?" Sam asked. "If they live around here, they'd likely know what he faced when he got to Crow City."

"I don't know," she said, "and of course I don't know where they live, but I've had a great deal to do with men and I know bad men when I see them. When I say bad, I don't mean men who hold up banks or forge checks. I mean men who are bad at heart, men who enjoy making someone else suffer. Believe me, I have had experience with men like that."

"I'm setting out to look for my Pa in the morning," Sam said, "but I don't know where to start because I don't know who they are or where they come from. I don't have no chance of finding him unless you can give me some help."

"Mr. Doyle said much the same thing," she said, "and I told him I can't give anybody any help. They had bandannas over their faces. Their clothes were the same as any cowboy would wear. Their guns were rifles and all three of them wore hand guns in their holsters."

She paused, frowning. "There is one thing I just now remembered. The man who took your father off, the one who stuck his gun and head into the coach, had a scar on the back of his right hand. It might have been made by a knife." She shook her head ruefully. "I'd like to help you, but that's the best I can do."

He rose. "Thank you, Miss Larkin. I'll think about that scar."

"You know my name," she said, as if surprised.

"I saw it on the register," he said.

"Then you know who my brother was."

He shook his head. "I don't think I do."

"Bud Larkin," she said. "The young man who was murdered by the invaders along with Lon Hale."

He was stunned. He asked, "You didn't know who my father was?"

She shook her head, smiling faintly. "I did not. I didn't ask his name and he didn't ask mine. You see, I've been in Alaska. I didn't know for a long time what had happened. Bud never wrote very often, so when I didn't hear from him for months at a time I never worried. I didn't know he had been killed until I picked up a Seattle newspaper that told about the invasion. It was months old. I left Alaska as soon as I could sell my business."

"Why did you sell your business and come here?"

"To find out what had happened, and about Mike Hale. I've wondered for a long time what kind of man he was. You see, Bud worshipped both Mike and Lon. I don't know why, except that they claimed to be his friends. I guess to Bud they were romantic cowboys, you know, knights of the plains or whatever crazy ideas a young man has who leaves home and comes west for adventure."

She paused, then added thoughtfully, "I'd like to know who was responsible for Bud's death. I'm not sure it really was your father and his friends. I'd like to talk to him. I would have if I'd known who he was. If Bud really had helped rustle cattle and steal horses, then I guess his killing was justified, for this country anyhow, but you see, he wasn't that kind of a boy as I remember him, so why did he go bad, if he did?"

"I'm sorry about him being killed," Sam said. "I didn't like the idea of the invasion. I fought with my pa about it, but the law in this county wasn't doing nothing to stop the rustling and horse stealing, so there was the other side to what happened."

She rose. "Mr. Powers, I want to go with you when you search for your father. I'm an excellent rider and I promise I won't slow you up."

He walked to the door, wondering what Betty would think of such an arrangement. "I'm sorry, Miss Larkin, but I can't let you do that. It's too dangerous."

She stood watching him as he let himself out of the room, a small, tantalizing smile on her lips. He went down the stairs, breathing hard and vaguely feeling that he had escaped from some unknown danger. When he reached the lobby, Doyle was still behind the desk.

"Why didn't you tell me she was Bud Larkin's sister?" Sam demanded.

"I figured you'd find out," Doyle said. "Now there's a woman. I never saw one like her."

"She scares me," Sam said. "She knows too much, but I'm not sure exactly what she knows, and I sure don't know why she's here."

"I'm guessing she came to kill Adam," Doyle said.

"She's been in Casper. She likely read in the paper that he was coming home."

"In that case it's a good thing she didn't know who he was," Sam said. "But why Pa? There's forty-nine others she might just as well kill."

"Not if you count out the Texas gunslingers who have already gone home," Doyle said. "Only about half of the fifty were Wyoming ranchers. Besides, your pa was a leader, and along with Seth Alexander he had the most publicity in the newspaper."

"If you find out any more about her, let me know," Sam said. "I'm guessing we're going to hear more about her before we're done."

He turned into the bar on the chance that Zeke Partridge was there. A crowd had gathered and Zeke was holding forth on how he didn't move a muscle during the holdup or he'd have been shot. It was the first time he had ever been held up and he hoped it was the last.

"I tell you, boys," Zeke said, "them Winchesters they was holding had the biggest damn barrels I ever seen, and the longer I sat there looking at 'em, the bigger they got."

Sam worked his way through the crowd until he reached the stage driver. He said, "Zeke, I got to find Pa. Can't you give me some idea who they were? Was there anything familiar about the man's voice?"

Zeke shook his head. "Sure can't, Sam. I don't even know if they live around here."

Sam left the hotel and strode along the board walk to where his horse was tied. He had never felt more frustrated in his life. He still didn't have the slightest idea where to start looking for his father.

Revenge At Crow City

can explain it to him, can't you? I ain't fixing to argue

Chapter 6

Tony Arbanz stood on the walk in front of the hotel until Main Street was empty. The homesteaders had gone home. Bronc Collins had left town in the buckboard. Jason Small had gone into his bank, Fred Ames into the store. Sam Powers was in the hotel. Arbanz was alone on the street except for a hungry-looking dog that was nosing around in front of the livery stable for something to eat.

This day had been the most disappointing day of Arbanz's life. It simply had not gone the way he had planned. He was thoroughly frustrated; he felt empty, drained out. He had been so sure that by now Adam Powers would be swinging from a limb of the big cottonwood by the creek. He had dreamed of it for months. Now, because of someone's stupid act, it had not happened. He believed Sam Powers when he said he'd had nothing to do with taking his father off the stage. He hadn't at first, but he did now. So who, then, had done it and why? He wished to hell he knew.

He crossed the street to his office, closed the door behind him, and sat down at his desk. He opened the second drawer on his right and took out a pile of papers. He turned slowly through the sheets, glancing at his handwriting. He had attempted to tell the story of the invasion right from the beginning and he was sure he had done a believable job. The public had a right to know, but it was unnecessary to look at the manuscript because he remembered exactly what had happened.

He had started working on the book the day after the invaders had been captured and interned at the fort. Now it was almost ready for printing. One more chapter would bring it up to date. He would be setting up the type in another week or so. He had been so sure that the last chapter would include the hanging of Adam Powers, a hanging that would certainly have been justified by the murder of Lon Hale and Bud Larkin. As he'd planned this, he had regretted that Seth Alexander wouldn't be here to hang alongside Powers, but Alexander was too smart to ever show his face in Bensen County.

Dropping the pile of paper back into the drawer, he pushed it shut and leaned back in his chair and closed his eyes. He remembered, all right. God, how well he remembered the last time he had been in the Cheyenne Club.

Two years ago it had been. That was it, just about two years ago. At the time he had been editor of the *Wyoming Stockman's Journal,* a job that had made him the spokesman for the cattle industry of Wyoming. The only fault he could find in himself was the fact that he had been gullible, and perhaps there was no excuse for that, but editing the *Journal* had been a good job and he had felt fortunate to have it.

For several years he had published articles and editorials that argued the side of the big cattlemen against the homesteaders, who had moved in like a plague of locusts and threatened the very life of the cattle industry. Being gullible, he had believed everything he was told about the homesteaders.

Before that last fatal day he had never been on the range for any length of time; he had never talked to a homesteader. He had been told they were all cattle rustlers and horse thieves who had filed on quarter sections of land simply as a front for their lawless activities.

He knew better now because he had made it a point to get acquainted with every homesteader who lived within twenty miles of Crow City. He had found that in general they were hard-working, God-fearing men who wanted to own their land, wanted it to the point that it became a compulsion and made them undergo

hardships that were unbelievable. There were a few
exceptions, men like Mike and Lon Hale, who probably
were cattle rustlers and horse thieves, but Arbanz was
sure there weren't many of them.

He had not known that then, and he wouldn't have
believed it if he had been told. He had been on the right
side, the governing side, the side with the power and
the money. He had been satisfied with his life. He had
hobnobbed with the big men of the state and was accepted as an equal. He'd eaten with them and he'd
drunk with them and he'd been invited out to their
ranches for barbecues and similar celebrations.

Well, he hadn't known it then, but it had been a
goddamned empty kind of life. He had accepted it as
the right life for him until he had been caught in a
snowslide of truth. Now he guessed he was a fanatic, a
zealot. He was no longer a follower, a lackey who did
what he was told; he was a leader.

Tony Arbanz was his own man now and he was
proud of it. He was in a small pond, but he was a hell
of a big frog in it, big enough to plan Adam Powers'
hanging. He would have brought it off if that mysterious
somebody had left Powers on the stagecoach.

His reversal of attitude had been a complete one
hundred eighty degrees. The day it happened had
started the same as any day. Betty had just finished at
the University of Wyoming, and he had been able to
pull a few wires, so she had landed a job in the
Cheyenne school system. He had lost his wife several
years before, and he had learned to take care of himself and the house when Betty was in school, but he
was glad to have her home. She had cooked breakfast for him that particular morning. He had shaved
and dressed and had gone to his office. Then he'd had
a telephone call to come to the Cheyenne Club.

When he reached the club, the doorman told him he
was expected in the conference room. He climbed the
stairs to the second floor, enjoying the smooth, sensual
feel of the white oak banister and the softness of the
thick carpet on the steps. His life had not been one

of poverty, but it had not been one of great luxury, either. He always enjoyed coming here for that reason, if for no other.

The conference room was in the front of the building and looked down upon the spacious lawn that was kept so immaculate that it resembled a green carpet. Many of the club members belonged to rich families from the eastern part of the United States and England. They were cattlemen only in the sense that they owned cattle ranches, but they seldom saw their outfits. They spent the bulk of their time in the club drinking or gambling, or at the racetrack, or just riding around on their high-wheeled bicycles.

The men who actually controlled the club were truly cattlemen, many having lived in Wyoming since the early days, and their talk about fighting Indians and outlaws for their land was true enough. Arbanz had listened to them for hours at a time and he had learned to admire them. They were the men who had actually tamed the land, and it seemed to him unfair that now the homesteaders could move in and take over the range after it was safe to come. This was the argument the cattlemen made and it had always seemed valid to Arbanz.

The door of the conference room was open and Arbanz entered without knocking. A dozen men sat around the long walnut table, suntanned men wearing high-heeled boots. Some lived in Laramie County, near Cheyenne; some, in Albany County, on the Laramie plains; others, on the North Platte and the Sweetwater; and Adam Powers lived in Bensen County, where the rustling and horse stealing had been the worst in the state for the last two years.

Colonel Seth Alexander was the chairman of the board of directors of the club. He was physically the biggest man in the club, the richest, the most powerful politically, and he owned the biggest spread in the state. He was also the most obnoxious, insisting on being called Colonel, although his credentials were dubious. He was ruthless, capable of simply rolling over anyone who had the temerity to oppose him. No one in the club did, Tony Arbanz least of all.

"Come in," Alexander boomed. "Sit down. We were waiting for you."

Arbanz closed the door and took the one vacant chair at the table, feeling that he had been reprimanded for not coming sooner, although he had dropped everything and come as soon as he got the message. He nodded at some of the others and sat back against the chair, feeling vaguely uneasy. He did not know why he had been summoned to a meeting of this kind. These were the big men of the cattle industry, a company that did not include him.

"Now then," Alexander said, "we'll get down to the business of the day. I don't need to go over the ground we are all familiar with, the condition of law enforcement in some counties, Bensen in particular. All of us know that another year or two of wide-open rustling will bankrupt us, and we know equally well that the sheriffs of several counties not only wink at rustling but may be a part of the thievery.

"We have talked about what measures can be taken to stop these crimes, and we have agreed that we have reached the point where we must take the law into our own hands or give up and move out of the state. None of us will do that. This meeting has been called to adopt such a policy and make plans to act upon it. Adam, will you explain what we have decided to do."

As Powers rose, Arbanz knew that Alexander and one or two more like Powers had already made the decision, that this meeting had been called as a matter of form to give a pretense of legality to the program. No one would object, at least openly, because every man here was used to this procedure.

Powers cleared his throat. "This plan will take some time, and we can't afford the time. We should have started this a year ago, but we couldn't make up our minds that the only way to solve our problem was to fight fire with fire.

"We're gonna take the war into Bensen County. It's

my county, and I can get more out of this than any of the rest of you, even though it's no secret that the goddamned thieves have just about broken me. I may be able to hang on to some of what I have if we get this plan moving fast enough, but it will take the help of every one of you, giving manpower or money, or both. Our thinking is that if we don't stop it now in Bensen County, we're going to have the same situation in every county in the state. In other words, if we make an example out of Bensen County, we'll stop the spread of the disease."

"Get on with it, Adam," Alexander said impatiently.

"Sure," Powers said. "We'll need fifty armed men, horses, a cook, a doctor, and a wagon and driver with supplies. Somebody ought to go to Texas right away to recruit twenty-five good men who can handle guns. We'll raise the other twenty-five in Wyoming, either owners or foremen, or top hands from our crews who can be trusted.

"We'll have a special car on the tracks here in Cheyenne and we'll move the Texas men into it as soon as they get here. Some of you will join the expedition here. We'll move the car to Casper and pick up other men and horses between here and Casper. The rest will join after we get there.

"I'll be the guide because it's my county. We'll leave Casper with our supplies as soon as possible and move north fast. I've made out a list of men we will execute when we get to Bensen County. There's forty-five names. These ain't just rustlers; they're businessmen in Crow City who helped the rustlers: a banker, the sheriff of Bensen County, a storekeeper, a lawyer who defends them in court, and some others. Soon's we've executed these men, we'll divide up into five groups, move out into all parts of Bensen County, and finish the executions."

He paused a moment, his glance moving around the circle of faces, then he added, "Some of you may think this is going too far, but believe me, the situation is desperate. We've tried everything else. And remember, Granville Stuart did this same thing a few years ago on the Yellowstone and the Missouri. You won't find a more popular man in Montana today than Granville Stuart."

Arbanz looked around the table in disbelief. No one argued. None of the men there showed the slightest expression of disagreement. They were deadly serious, morally and mentally accepting Powers' proposal as if it were a reasonable solution to the problem. Hanging a rustler or a horse thief caught in the act was one thing; invading a county with fifty armed men and hanging everyone who was on Adam Powers' list was something else. It was wholesale murder, and nothing that Alexander or Powers or anyone else could say changed that fact.

Still, Arbanz might not have said anything in the meeting if Alexander had not looked at him and said, "You may be wondering why we called you in, Arbanz, since you are not personally involved in the cattle business. However, you are our spokesman. The *Journal* not only goes to practically every stock grower in the state, but it also goes to other people as well and even has considerable circulation outside the state.

"Your job will be to recruit public opinion, which I'm afraid we will need to make this mission a success. In other words, we don't want this to seem like thoughtless killing on our part. Actually we represent the law, which is being ignored by local sheriffs and deputies. I can assure you that the men who run the state government in Cheyenne are on our side. You will begin immediately to demand serious action, and later pick up that demand until the readers assume that what we do is in response to this demand. We will have the press on our side, but . . ."

Arbanz could not stand any more. It was bad enough to be brought here to listen to their plotting, but to be made a part of the conspiracy of murder was too much. He got to his feet and gripped the table, trembling.

"Sir," he shouted loud enough to be heard above Alexander's booming bass, "I will have no part of this. It is murder and you can't make anything else out of it. You are not trying these men you propose to hang. You are taking Mr. Powers' word for who is a rustler. You intend to lynch men who have committed no crime greater than being sympathetic to the homesteaders' cause. As long as the *Journal* is in my hands, it will not condone murder."

Alexander and Powers stood frozen, their eyes on him. They were too shocked by this rebellion from such an unexpected source to say or do anything for several seconds. Then Alexander bellowed, "Then, by God, the *Journal* is not in your hands. You're fired."

"Good," Arbanz said, and started toward the door.

He was halfway across the room, his back to the men, when he was struck by a powerful blow on the back of the neck that knocked him to the floor. Half-conscious, he heard Powers say, "We ought to kill the bastard."

Someone kicked him in the ribs; he never knew whether it was Alexander or Powers. Then Alexander hauled him to his feet and shook him. Alexander said in a tone unusually low for him, "If you ever mention this to anyone else, you are a dead man." Alexander shook him again. "Savvy?"

Arbanz was conscious enough to nod. Alexander opened the door and shoved him through it. He sprawled on the thick hall carpet that he had always admired. He lay there for a time, unable to move. He finally crawled to the head of the stairs, pulled himself upright, and slowly made his way down the stairs, hanging to the white oak banister.

He was breathing easier by the time he reached the lobby. He walked slowly to the front door and left the clubhouse, saying nothing to the doorman, who stared at him curiously. He trudged home, though afterwards he had little memory of that slow and painful walk.

When he reached his house, he told Betty what had happened, then said he had to get out of town, that they would kill him if he stayed. He was going to Bensen County and either buy the newspaper that was there or start a new one. Betty was to stay and sell the house, then join him. She'd have to resign her teaching position in Cheyenne, but she could probably get another one in or around Crow City.

When he reached Crow City, he found that the editor of the *Sentinel* had had enough of the growing terror in Bensen County and was glad to find a buyer. Through the following months Arbanz repeatedly told the story of what the cattlemen planned to do, but very few believed it. As time went on, however, more and more people did accept what he said about an approaching armed invasion.

He had hoped to stop it. He had failed in that, but his constant hammering on what was to come did prepare the homesteaders and townsmen for what actually happened. They rose as one man to fight off the invaders. In that he had succeeded.

Through these years his hatred for Alexander and Powers grew rather than diminished. He never saw Alexander again, but he saw Powers on Crow City's main street a number of times. He had started wearing a gun, not knowing what Adam Powers would do, but the cowman never attempted to harm him. They simply passed each other on the street, each pretending not to know the other.

He was startled from his thoughts by the opening of the front door. He straightened up in his chair, rubbed his face with his hands, and shook his head. He seldom allowed himself to become so deeply immersed in the past, but his frustration over the failure to hang Adam Powers had brought it all back.

Mike Hale had come in. Arbanz called, "Howdy,

Mike," and got up from his chair. He didn't know Hale very well and didn't care to. He never wanted to be put in the position of having to defend the man in the *Sentinel*. It was men like Hale who had brought on the invasion. He should have been sent to the state pen years ago.

"Howdy, Tony," Hale said. "I was wondering if you ever found out what happened to old man Powers. I came to town expecting to see him swinging in the breeze the way he deserved, but hell, he never showed up."

"I don't know any more than you do," Arbanz said. "He just wasn't on that stage."

"He was supposed to be, wasn't he?" Hale asked.

Arbanz nodded. "That was the word we got from Casper."

"Maybe Sam took him off," Hale said. "He knew the old man was coming, didn't he?"

"Ed Garber told him," Arbanz said, "but he swears he knows nothing about what happened."

"Probably lying," Hale said carelessly. "Well, we'll get another chance at the old bastard one of these days."

He turned and walked out. Arbanz, watching him cross the street to his horse, asked himself, *Now what was that all about?*

Chapter 7

When Sam got back to the AP, supper was ready. He pumped water into the basin that was on a stand near the back door, then joined his mother and Bronc

Collins at the table. His mother wasn't crying, but her eyes were red, so he knew she had been.

He didn't say anything until he had filled his plate. Then he said, "I reckon Bronc told you what happened."

Ida Powers nodded. "I don't know what to think. I feel guilty because I really didn't want Adam to ever come back; then when I heard he was coming, I knew I had to make the most of it. I got the house all ready for him, and now I wonder if he will ever be here."

"I sure don't know," Sam said. "Nobody has any more idea about who took Pa off the stage than I do, or why he was taken. I talked to Zeke, the drummer who was on the stage, and the woman. Oh, her name is Julie Larkin. She's a sister to Bud Larkin, who was killed with Lon Hale."

Startled, Mrs. Powers asked, "What in the world is she doing here?"

"I don't rightly know," Sam said. "She told me she had been in Alaska and didn't know what had happened to Bud. She came as soon as she could sell her business."

"What kind of business was it?" Mrs. Powers said.

"She didn't say," Sam answered, "but she's an uncommon woman. Pretty and expensive, I'd say from the clothes she was wearing, but I couldn't figure her. I just felt uneasy when I was talking to her. I guess I knew I wasn't a match for her." He thought about it a moment, not sure why he felt the way he did about her, then added, "Seemed like I was a country boy and she had been everywhere and seen everything."

"Could she have had anything to do with Adam being taken off the stage?" Mrs. Powers asked.

"She claimed she didn't know who he was." Sam looked at Bronc. "She did give me one clue. She said the man who did the talking and shoved his gun barrel into the coach had a scar on the back of his hand. You know of anybody around here who qualifies?"

45

"What did he look like?" Bronc asked.

"They were masked," Sam said, "so nobody got a look at their faces, but I did learn that the one who did the talking was short and heavy-set."

Bronc sipped his coffee, frowning thoughtfully. "I can't think of nobody but Mike Hale. He got a knife cut across the back of one hand in a fight in the Casino last winter. You know how Hale is. If he don't have a fight, he looks for one, only that time he got the worst of it."

"Who was he fighting with?"

Bronc shrugged. "Some hard case. I didn't know him. Probably another member of the Red Sash gang. They scrap among themselves a lot."

"I hadn't thought of Hale," Sam said, "but it could have been him, all right. He hates Pa. Always has, just like Pa hated him, only it'd be worse now after his brother got killed."

Bronc shook his head. "I dunno. Seems like he'd have wanted Adam to come on into town. He knowed what they'd do with Adam if they got their hands on him."

"Yeah, looks like he would," Sam agreed, "but he's always after a dollar. Maybe he figures we'll pay a ransom, and chances are we'll never see Pa if we do."

"If that's it," Mrs. Powers said, "you'll have to pay what he asks."

Sam didn't say anything, but he knew more about the family finances than his mother did. There just wasn't much cash in the bank. Jason Small would make a loan, but it probably wouldn't be enough. Besides, Adam had always been adamantly opposed to mortgaging the AP. If he was saved by ransom obtained from mortgaging the ranch, he'd give Sam hell for doing it.

When he finished, Sam rose. "I'm going over to see Betty. It's time we had a showdown with Tony. Besides, he might know something about Hale."

"Arbanz ain't one to help you find Adam," Bronc grunted.

"I think he might," Sam said. "He still wants to hang Pa."

"I thought he promised to shoot you if you showed up over there," his mother said.

"He did," Sam said. "I aim to see if he's bluffing. I stopped on my way home and saw Betty. She's expecting me. She'll see he don't shoot straight."

He clapped his hat on his head and went out into the thin evening light. By the time he had saddled up and ridden to the Arbanz place, it was dusk. He dismounted in front of the house and tied his horse, then remained motionless beside the hitch rail. He was not surprised a moment later when a rifle cracked and a bullet kicked up dust at his side.

"All right, Tony," Sam called as he raised his hands above his head. "I got your invitation to leave, but I'm coming in, so put your Winchester down."

He walked directly toward the front door, his hands held high. The rifle cracked again, but this time there was no sign of a bullet. Arbanz let out an angry yell and swore. "Damn it, Betty, I'd have fixed him that time. What'd you knock my rifle barrel down for?"

"That question is about as stupid as what you're trying to do," Betty said furiously. "Come in here, Sam, and knock some sense into my father's head if you can. At least take the Winchester away from him."

Sam grinned as he stepped into the living room. Arbanz was standing about ten feet inside the door, still clutching his rifle, but Betty had forced the barrel down and kept it there. She was a strong woman and nearly as tall as her father, so he was not having much luck freeing the rifle. Apparently his second shot had gone into the floor.

"You've had your say," Sam said as he gripped Arbanz's wrists and yanked them away from the rifle. "Now sit down before I do knock some sense into your head."

Arbanz sat down in a rocking chair as Betty put the rifle back on the antler rack near the front door. He wiped his face with a bandanna, then muttered, "Hell, I could have nailed you with my first shot. I guess I should have."

"You're all bluff, Tony," Sam said as he sat down on the couch. "You've been making mean noises about me for months, but I don't think you ever did aim to kill me."

"Sure I did," Arbanz flared. "I'd kill you rather than have the only child I've got marry the son of Adam Powers."

"I'm not a child," Betty snapped. "That's the whole trouble. You still think of me as a child, but I'm over twenty-one and I have a right to make my own decisions and marry the man I love."

Arbanz looked at his daughter for a long time. Sam was surprised at the expression of tenderness that was on the man's face. He had always seemed to Sam a violent, feisty man incapable of experiencing any of the softer, warm emotions, but there could be no mistaking the feeling that was gripping him now. For the first time Sam felt compassion for him.

"I know you're not a child," Arbanz said finally, "and I know you have a right to make your own decisions, but I love you and I want what is best for you."

"Then let me marry Sam and give us your blessing," she said. "If I have to choose between you and Sam, I'll choose Sam."

He was hurt by that. He folded his hands and stared at the floor, a pulse beating in his forehead, two spots of red appearing in his cheeks.

"I'd rather have your blessings than a bullet from your gun," Sam said. "I guess you ain't looked at yourself very close, Tony. You got no reason to hate me. You hate Pa, so you think you've got to hate me, but I'm not responsible for what Pa did. I guess it's wrong, but the truth is I've hated Pa, too, a lot of times. So has Ma. He's the kind of man it's easy to hate."

Arbanz tipped his head back and stared at Sam. "I had no idea you felt that way," he said. "I guess you're right. I don't have any reason to hate you, but there is another thing. I don't want Betty to be a rancher's wife and work the way your mother has had to do. Half starve, too, I gather from what I've heard the last year or two. She deserves better."

"I'm not afraid of work," Betty said sharply. "I guess this is the time to make everything plain. Sam and I will get married as soon as the trouble about his father is settled. I will either move into his mother's house or we will build a small house on the AP. I know you'll need a housekeeper, but you'll have to hire one or do your own housework."

"I did it when you were in college," Arbanz said. "I can do it again."

"And I want to say one more thing now that we've got it in the open," Sam said. "I don't blame you for feeling the way you do about Pa and Seth Alexander and the rest. You've got plenty of reason."

Arbanz wiped a hand across his face. "Well now, I'm surprised at that, too. I'm ashamed of myself for editing the *Journal* as long as I did, fawning over those bastards and enjoying the prestige of being with big men of the state. I never had my eyes open until that day they started talking about the invasion and taking it for granted that I'd go along and continue to be their yes man. The Cheyenne ring has got to be exposed, and I've been doing my best to get the job done."

"I'm for that," Sam agreed. "They're not done, either, and if you'd hung Pa, you'd have brought martial law down on Bensen County. I think that's all it would take for Alexander and his friends to prove to the governor that we're as lawless as we ever were."

"Then it will be civil war," Arbanz said ominously. "We'll have a lot more killing than the invasion brought about."

"I'm sure of that," Sam agreed. "What I really came over for tonight was to talk about Pa's kidnapping. Do you have any idea who did it or why, now you've had time to think about it?"

Arbanz shook his head. "No, I don't. I haven't had

a chance to talk to anyone since I saw you this afternoon except Mike Hale and I didn't learn anything from him."

"How did you happen to be talking to Mike Hale?" Sam asked.

"He came into the office," Arbanz said. "Wanted to know if I'd heard anything about your father."

"Did you ever think Hale might be the one who took Pa off that stage?" Sam asked.

Arbanz was startled. "No. Why would he?"

"He had about as much reason as anybody," Sam said, "with his brother getting killed. I'm wondering if any of the rest of the Red Sash gang was involved."

"You don't even know that Hale is a member," Arbanz said. "I never saw him with a sash on."

"Which don't prove nothing," Sam said. "I'm going to get Ed Garber in the morning and we'll ride out to see Hale. Of course, he won't have Pa on his place, and it's a big country out there, so I don't reckon we'll find anything."

"Adam may not even be alive," Arbanz said. "Did you think of that?"

"I thought of it, all right," Sam said. "I'm hoping that Hale has a ransom in mind. If he does, he may keep Pa alive."

He rose and turned to the door. Arbanz said, "If I hear anything, I'll let you know."

Sam nodded and left the room, Betty following. Outside she caught up with him and held his arm as they walked into the darkness. When they reached his horse, she said, "I don't know that we changed Daddy's mind. He's a stubborn man. He always has been."

"Nothing's changed with us, has it?" Sam asked. "I think we'll know about Pa in a couple of days."

"Nothing's changed," she said. "We'll get married any day you say."

He kissed her and she clung to him for a moment, then she said, "Maybe I hate him, too, Sam, but he's the only father I have."

Chapter 8

Adam Powers rode with his captors directly east from the kidnap scene except where steep-walled gullies or sharply sloped hills forced them to circle. Adam knew this part of the range as well as he knew his front yard, but now it looked different. Then he thought that it was because he hadn't seen it for so long.

He saw a dozen or more cows to the north, but he couldn't tell whether they carried the AP brand or not. A few years ago there would have been no doubt. His cattle were all over the country, but he guessed the ones he saw weren't his. Sam and Bronc probably kept the few hundred head they still owned close to headquarters, where they could be watched.

Much of this land had been taken by homesteaders, but by now most of the claims had been deserted. They passed a number of shacks and dugouts, but only two showed signs of life. Still, the settlers had stayed long enough to plow up much of the grass, leaving gray patches surrounded by green.

Nature would take years to heal the scars the homesteaders had made. This land was never meant to be farmed, he told himself, as he had hundreds of times, and only a stupid ignorant government in Washington would ever have opened it for homesteading in the first place. But just try to tell that to the government. He and Seth Alexander and other cowmen had tried hard enough.

Today for some reason the old bitterness refused to return. He remembered how he had felt before the invasion, wanting to hang every homesteader in Bensen County for destroying the grass, and the land, too, because much of the topsoil had been lost to the dry winds.

The land that was good for farming lay close to the Big Horns, where the settlers could irrigate from the streams that boiled down from the mountains. The men who had settled there had made it, and in all fairness Adam could not fault them. They were the ones who had made the town of Crow City possible. But the men who tried to dry farm the eastern part of the county were spoilers, fools who had let the land locators take advantage of them.

Well, he guessed that the past year of failure and frustration and being held prisoner at the forts had mellowed him. Too, he had a feeling of death. Mike Hale would never let him go home. Now, suddenly and unexpectedly, tears rolled down his cheeks. He would never see Ida or Sam again. Nor old Bronc Collins, who had been as loyal as any man could be.

He wiped a sleeve across his eyes, feeling like a fool. He couldn't remember crying before in his life, at least not since he'd been a small child. He had always prided himself on being a hard man, a man who never showed any emotion, but he was feeling it now and showing it. He couldn't help it. A sign of age, he told himself.

The kid behind him jeered, "What's the matter, Gramps? Hurting somewhere? Got a saddle sore already?"

"Got some dust in my eye," he said.

The lanky man in front looked back. "It ain't much farther," he said, "and then you'll get a chance to rest for a long time."

"Yeah, a hell of a long time," the kid said in the same jeering tone.

The lanky man and the kid looked a good deal alike, and Adam guessed they were father and son. He had never seen either of them before and he wondered where Mike Hale got them. They were probably members of the Red Sash gang that had stolen him blind. He didn't know much about the outfit except that they were horse thieves and rustlers, and were well organized, stealing here, then moving the cattle and horses to places where they could be disposed of.

He guessed that the sheriff, Ed Garber, was a member of the gang, but he had no way of proving that. Garber had never arrested any of them, but maybe he was just incompetent. The old sheriff would have smashed the gang in a matter of weeks. He'd been tough and mean, and some said a killer, but by God, he'd been a hell of a lawman.

They reached the canyon of the Dry Fork and the lanky man motioned to the kid, who swung to the north and then turned east. "This is it," the lanky man said, and nodded for Adam to put his horse down the steep slope to the bottom of the ravine.

Adam didn't know exactly where Hale lived, but he knew it wasn't far from here. Hale had not been among the first who homesteaded in Bensen County. He'd had a good thing going with his brother Lon somewhere to the south on the North Platte until Seth Alexander had run them out of the country. By the time they rode into Bensen County, the best land had been taken.

Adam didn't know why Mike and his brother Lon had split up, but the rumor was that they had disagreed about where to settle, so Lon had thrown in with the Larkin kid and had settled in the south end of the county. Mike had come farther north and had filed on his claim.

Adam had spent a lot of time hunting for Hale and would have strung him up on general principles if he'd caught him, but the man was elusive. In any case, Adam said there was no use going to his cabin after a herd of cattle had been stolen. That was the one place where he wouldn't be, but Sam, along with several of the AP hands, had found his cabin and had spent several days watching, but Hale never showed up.

They reached the bottom of the ravine and turned downstream. A few minutes later they came to a clump of cottonwoods that grew close to the north bank. The lean man reined up and motioned for Adam to dismount.

"This is gonna be your home for a while," the lanky man said. "Probably for the rest of your life. It ain't much for a man of your taste, but there's candles and matches on the table, some grub on the shelves, and wood for a fire. You'll make out."

Adam dismounted, finding that he was stiffer than he had expected. It had been a long time since he had been on a horse. The lean man had moved through the cottonwoods and opened a door that led into a dugout. The wood was weathered so the door looked little different from the dirt on both sides of it. A man riding by would not be likely to notice it unless he had his attention called to it.

"In here," the lanky man said, motioning for Adam to enter the dugout. "You've got about twenty feet on both sides of the door to walk if you want to, but don't go any farther than that. My boy Jerry is up there on top with his Winchester. He ain't never killed a man, but he wants to, so don't give him no excuse to make you the first one."

Adam looked up at the top of the steep slope above him. He saw the kid hunkered down with his Winchester across his knees. When he saw Adam staring up at him, he waved. He'd probably kill him just for the sake of killing a man, Adam thought. Lank knew his boy, all right.

"Get in here," the lanky man ordered. "See if there's anything you need."

Adam stepped into the dugout. He'd seen plenty of them from the outside, but he'd never been in one before and he had never thought he would be. The fetid smell was sickening. It was more than stale air. Probably some animal had crawled in here and died. Adam hesitated, thinking he was going to throw up. Just the thought of spending the rest of his life in this dugout, for months or even a few short hours, was more than he could bear.

He wheeled and ran toward the horse he had been riding. The kid's rifle cracked, the bullet kicking up dust in front of him. Apparently the lanky man had expected something like this because he overtook Adam before he reached the horse, grabbed him by a shoulder, and shook him.

"Damn it, I told you what would happen if you tried to run," the lanky man said. "It's a wonder Jerry didn't kill you."

He whirled Adam around and propelled him back into the dugout. "I don't blame you for not cottoning to your new home, or even wanting to get yourself killed, but I don't figure on letting that happen. Mike would take my hide off with a dull knife if I did."

He gave Adam a shove that sent him sprawling back across a bunk. He fell on his stomach, the wind jolted out of him. He lay motionless for a time, fighting for breath.

"You'll get used to the stink after a while," the lanky man said. "I'm going to lock you up now. I figured on leaving the door open so you'd get some fresh air, but after that fool trick you just pulled, I see I can't do it."

He stepped outside and closed the door. Adam turned over on his back. There was just a thin line of light around the door. He put his hands out beside him and felt of the mattress. It was straw. Below it were boards. Just damned hard boards. He'd been bothered by rheumatism for several weeks. This would make it worse.

He crossed the room to the door and shoved on it. It didn't budge. He shoved harder, but there was still no give; he backed up and slammed a shoulder against it. All he did was to hurt his shoulder. The door was rock solid. He felt around in the darkness until he found the table, then searched for matches, found them, and struck one. A candle stood upright in a nearby cup. He held the flame to the wick, then blew out the match.

The small flame did little to dispell the darkness. He

moved around the edge of the dugout, kicking at the dirt walls and running his hand along them. It was just as he knew it would be. He was in a cave dug back into the side of the cliff, and the only way out was through the door that was locked.

He moved around the dugout again, searching for something that he could dig with or use to hammer against the door. There was nothing. He blew the candle out and put it back on the table, then felt his way to the bunk. He lay down and thought about his situation.

He could see no hope whatever, and now, for the first time in his life, he thought about what it was like to die. Oh, sure, he was an old man and had known for months that death was not far away, but this was different. It was close. Mike Hale would kill him slowly and painfully. Letting him starve to death in this goddamned cave might be the way he'd do it.

Chapter 9

Tony Arbanz slept very little after Sam Powers left. He lay on his back, staring into the darkness, the pattern of his thoughts turned bitter. He told himself he was a failure. Crow City needed a newspaper, all right, and he had given the town a good one. The point was that he had let his hate dominate him, govern every thought and action, and when he had heard that Adam Powers was returning, he had been sure that he would accomplish something at last with the hanging of the old man who had been as much responsible as anyone for the invasion.

He had no hope now that Adam was alive, or that he would return to Crow City if he were. His thoughts turned to Betty, and he realized how much he had taken her for granted. Instead of wasting his time and emotions on hanging Adam Powers, he should have been doing something for his daughter.

Sam said that Arbanz hated him because he hated Sam's father. The boy was dead right. Arbanz had no reason whatever to hate Sam. He guessed, when it came right down to it, that he couldn't think of anyone he'd rather have for a son-in-law than Sam Powers.

"No, being in love isn't wrong." He'd patted her

When Betty had come in after Sam had left, she'd walked up to where he was sitting and put an arm around his shoulders. She'd said, "I'm sorry we had love is wrong."

to do this, Daddy, but we couldn't go on the way we were, not letting you know we were meeting and being afraid all the time you'd catch us and do something to Sam. We never did anything wrong, unless being in hand, and added, "It's all right, Betty. I was never one to admit I'd made a mistake, but that's what I've got to do this time. Sam's a fine young man. You have my blessing. Marry him tomorrow if you can."

She'd started to cry. When she could speak, she'd said, "I never thought I'd hear you say that."

He'd done something right at last, he told himself. He'd be a lonely man with Betty gone, but he'd get used to it. The trouble was, he'd let hate direct him for so long that now he faced an aimless life. Well, he'd have to find something to live for. His book might be enough. He'd finish it and get it published. Maybe, just maybe, it would change everything in Wyoming if he got it out before the next election.

He dropped off to sleep, but he woke an hour later, the first rays of the sun slipping through the east window of his bedroom. He lay there a few minutes, thinking he would drop off to sleep again, but he didn't. Restless, he rose, dressed and shaved, and slipped out of the house into the cool, winey air of early morning. He'd get breakfast in the hotel dining room.

The dining room was not open when Arbanz first entered the lobby. He glanced at his watch, saw that he had about ten minutes to wait, and sat down in a worn leather chair. Picking up a ragged copy of the Laramie *Boomerang,* he glanced at the headlines. It was an old paper that told about Bensen County running out of money and the release of the prisoners who had been held at Fort D. A. Russell.

The news story seemed to hint that this was justice at last, that it had been little short of criminal to hold some of the outstanding cowmen in the state prisoner all these months. Now Seth Alexander would be returning to his ranch on the North Platte, Adam Powers would be returning to Bensen County, and so on through a list of a dozen or more names.

He threw the paper across the room and swore softly. John Doyle had just entered the lobby. He moved behind the desk, smiling. He asked, "What's the matter, Tony? It's too early in the morning to be that mad."

"The press in the state has been on the side of the big ranchers from the beginning," Arbanz said. "You wonder what they'd have to do to change some editors' minds. If murder didn't do it, what would?"

The smile left Doyle's face. "I reckon you're one voice crying out in the wilderness," he said.

"One," Arbanz said. "Just one."

The door into the dining room had just opened. He rose and started toward the door, not wanting to get into an argument with Doyle. He knew what the hotel man thought, and he saw no point in trying to change his attitude. If the actual invasion had not altered the man's feeling, words wouldn't change it now.

He took a table near a street window and picked up the menu. He seldom ate breakfast here, so he read what was available, then gave his order of bacon, eggs, and coffee to the girl who had come to his table. He sat staring through the window into the dusty street, empty at this hour except for a shepherd dog that was wandering aimlessly along the dust strip.

He was not aware that a woman had approached his table until she said, "You are Mr. Tony Arbanz, the editor of the *Sentinel,* aren't you?"

Startled, he looked up into the face of a very attractive woman. She stood smiling down at him, her dark brown eyes alive with the love of life. She was young, probably about Betty's age, and quite small, not more than five feet two inches tall. She was wearing a white blouse. Her jacket was open, disclosing the tight pressure of her firm breasts.

He rose, nodding, "I'm Arbanz." He motioned to the chair across from him. "Will you sit down?"

"Thank you," she said as she took the chair. "I was hoping you would invite me to share your table. You are one of the reasons I came to Crow City. I would have gone to your office, but I'm happy to meet you here and to have a chance to talk to you. Mr. Doyle told me who you were."

She extended her hand across the table. "I should introduce myself. I'm Julie Larkin."

He thought of Bud Larkin, who had been murdered by the invaders, but there was probably no connection between him and this woman. He gripped her soft, warm hand and leaned back, his eyes on her. She was beyond doubt the most beautiful woman he had seen for years.

"What can I do for you, Miss Larkin?" he asked.

"First of all, I'm hungry," she said. "I'd like to order breakfast before we talk. As a matter of fact, I'm never very alert before I have my first cup of coffee in the morning."

Arbanz motioned for the waitress. When she came to the table, he said, "Miss Larkin wants to order breakfast."

"I must have my coffee," Julie said. "I'll want some toast, too, but bring the coffee at once."

The waitress nodded and disappeared into the kitchen. Julie said, "It was a long, hard ride from Casper and I guess I'm just tired this morning. Then there was the kidnapping of that old man. I certainly didn't expect anything like that."

Arbanz clapped a hand against his forehead. "I should have known," he said. "You're the young lady who came in on the stage yesterday."

"That's right," she said. "I understand I just missed a hanging. I think it would have been worse to have seen that than the kidnapping."

"Yes, it would," he said.

She motioned toward his plate. "Please eat your breakfast. It's getting cold."

He nodded and started to eat, but he had difficulty keeping his gaze from Julie's face. He had always been suspicious of beautiful women, and with conditions what they were in Bensen County, he had reason to be suspicious of any strangers. But there was an innocence about Julie Larkin that made it hard to believe he had any reason to be suspicious of her.

The waitress brought Julie's coffee. She had continued to smile at Arbanz, a warm and inviting smile that seemed to set the two of them apart from the rest of the world. When the coffee came, she spooned sugar into it and stirred, but she did not seem as desperate for it as she had sounded.

"I thought you would ask what the second reason was for my coming to Crow City," she said, "but since you didn't, I'll tell you anyway. I'm Bud Larkin's sister. I hoped to find out something more about his death than what I know, which is just about zero."

Arbanz took a long breath. So there was a connection between the woman and Bud Larkin. He said, "Does that have anything to do with your wanting to see me?"

"Only indirectly," she answered, and began to sip her coffee. "First, what can you tell me about Bud's death?"

"He was murdered by the invaders who planned to hang almost all of us who live in Crow City," he said, "but I guess you know that."

60

She nodded. "I know the bare facts of his death," she said, "and that he had a partner named Lon Hale, who was killed with him. What I want to know is whether he really was involved with cattle rustling."

"I can't answer that," Arbanz said. "I don't think anyone knows for sure. He was never tried and convicted; therefore, we have to presume he was not guilty."

"I would like to think that," she said thoughtfully. "Where is he buried?"

"In the cemetery here in Crow City," he said.

"Someday I'll have you show me his grave," she said, "but there's plenty of time for that."

The waitress brought Julie's toast. Arbanz had finished eating. He picked up his coffee cup and leaned back in his chair, watching Julie as she delicately nibbled at her toast. She was a real lady, he thought, and wondered where she came from and what she had been doing. He also wondered why it had taken her a year to come to Crow City to ask about her brother.

"Why don't you tell me what you wanted to see me about?" he asked. "I have to get over to the shop in a few minutes."

"Of course," she said. "I was in Cheyenne just before coming here. I read about the invasion and how you came here from Cheyenne and took the newspaper and fought for the settlers. It was not only noble of you, Tony, but . . ." She paused, and arched her brows. "May I call you Tony? I feel that I know you very well and I think we're going to know each other better."

"Of course," he said.

"It was also very brave," she went on. "You would, from all I've heard, have been one of the first ones lynched if the invaders had succeeded in doing what they planned, simply because you knew too much about their plotting. You must know more about the whole terrible business than anyone else."

"I think I do," he said, "and as for being lynched,

I could feel my neck stretching when I heard how close they were to Crow City."

"I want you to write a book about what happened," she said, "and why you came to Crow City in the first place. Also how you felt, because you are the real hero of the whole ugly drama. I can promise you publication and proper advertising and distribution of your book. I can also promise that we will sell thousands of copies."

He had stopped breathing, his coffee cup held in front of his face, a feeling of unreality coming over him. This was the kind of thing he had wished for, but he had never had any real hope of seeing it become reality.

"I've already written it," he said, "all but the last chapter, and it won't take me long to do that."

"You've already written it," she said, as if surprised and pleased. "Why, Tony, that's wonderful. That will save a lot of time, and time is important. We should get the book out immediately, while people are still talking about the Bensen County war."

He set his cup down, angry with himself for telling her he had actually written the book. He had told no one except Betty, because he had been afraid that the cattlemen would find some way to destroy it and perhaps murder him to keep him from rewriting it. Now he had blurted it out to a stranger.

"Why are you interested in this book?" he asked.

"Oh, I'm sorry," she said. "I left out the most important point." She finished her toast, drank the last of her coffee, and wiped her fingers on her napkin. "You see, I'm a field representative of the publishing house of Stafford and Buel. I'm authorized to offer you a contract if I like what you've done. Of course, I didn't know you had written the book, but I hoped to get you started and to stay here in Crow City until you had enough of it done for me to see how well you wrote."

She rose. He got up, slowly because he was stunned by what she had said. She had given him the answer to the question that had bothered him from the day he had started the book. How was he going to distribute the books to the booksellers and advertise them? He was completely ignorant about the business. He could write it and print it and have it bound in Cheyenne or Denver, but beyond that, he was lost.

He followed her into the lobby, stopping at the desk to pay for their breakfasts. She had paused near the foot of the stairs and stood looking back at him, her expression an inviting one of anticipation as he walked toward her. He wondered if she wanted to talk more about the book, but as he approached her, he had a sudden feeling that his writing was not what was uppermost in her mind.

When he reached her, she laid a hand on his arm, saying, "Wouldn't you like to come up to my room?"

He knew then what she was thinking about. His first inclination was to turn her down; then the thought of possessing this beautiful woman was too much.

"I would like that very much," he said.

Her smile deepened as she took his arm and they started up the stairs together. She said, "I had been looking forward to meeting you so much and hoping we would get to know each other well. We're going to, Tony. We're going to know each other very well."

Chapter 10

Sam saddled up after breakfast and rode into Crow City. He didn't say anything to his mother, except that he was going to spend the day looking for his father, but he told Bronc Collins he'd get some action out of Ed Garber or break his neck.

He stopped at the sheriff's office in the courthouse, but Garber wasn't there. The deputy said he didn't know where Garber was, probably home in bed. As Sam turned toward the door, the deputy said, "I got back to town too late for the excitement. What happened?"

"Ask Tony Arbanz," Sam said. "Or Jason Small. Or Fred Ames."

He strode back to his horse, mounted, and rode to the Garber house, a small frame building that Garber had bought after being elected sheriff. Before that he'd been just another homesteader who had been starved out dry farming east of town.

Garber had had no experience or training as a lawman, but he'd been the only member of the homesteader faction who wanted the job, so he was elected. Since then he had done as little as possible, and absolutely nothing as far as enforcing the law against the homesteaders. His one moment of glory had been when he'd rallied the settlers and townsmen as soon as word was received that the invaders were on their way to Crow City.

Sam dismounted and, letting his reins drag, strode up the path, stepped across the porch, and hammered on the front door. When no one answered, the pounded again. A moment later Mrs. Garber opened the door and stood scowling at Sam. She was wearing a robe, her hair was disheveled, and she was rubbing her eyes as if having trouble getting them open.

"You don't have to knock the door down," she snapped. "What do you want?"

"Ed."

"He ain't here."

She started to shut the door in his face, but he pushed past her into the living room. She screamed, "You can't just bull your way in here like this. You get out."

He didn't stop to argue, but stalked across the living room to the bedroom door and banged it open. Garber was in bed and apparently had been asleep. Now he reared up, demanding, "What the hell . . ."

The morning was cool and he was covered by a quilt. Sam grabbed a handful of the guilt and yanked it off the bed. Garber was naked. Sam took him by the ankles and pulled him off the bed. He hit the floor in a jarring crash. He bellowed an oath, scrambled to his feet, and plunged toward his gun, which was in a holster on his bureau top, but Sam, who was between him and the gunbelt, jerked it out of his reach.

"What the goddamned hell, Powers." Garber sat back on the bed. "Have you gone loco?"

"No. I'm just seeing that you earn your salary today."

"You bet I will," Garber shouted. "I'm arresting you for forcing your way into my home and assaulting an officer of the law and for trespassing."

"Oh, shut up," Sam said testily. "Get your clothes on. You're late getting to work, especially on a morning after a kidnapping. We're going after Mike Hale."

Garber's mouth dropped open. "What do we want Hale for?"

"For kidnapping my father," Sam answered. "We're going out to Hale's place and look for Pa."

"Oh no, we ain't," Garber said. "Hale's a dangerous man. If you've got solid evidence against him, I'll round up a posse and you can ride with us. Otherwise I ain't . . ."

"You better listen to me," Sam said, his legs spread, his hands fisted. "I never liked you much because you ain't worked at being sheriff, and when you do, it's a mighty one-sided job, but this time it's going to be different. You're coming with me and we're asking Hale some questions and we'll search his place or I'll give you a beating so your wife won't recognize you."

Garber swallowed and shook his head. "You son of a bitch. I believe you'd do it, but afterward I'd arrest you and throw you into the jug and let you rot."

"I don't think so," Sam said.

"Why?"

"Because you'd be dead."

Garber swallowed again and tried to stare Sam down, but he failed. He lowered his gaze and reached for his clothes, which were on a chair beside the bed. When he was dressed, Sam handed him his gunbelt. Garber buckled it around him, his eyes narrowed as he stared at Sam.

"Don't try it," Sam said. "I want you alive to give me a hand with Hale."

Garber shrugged and stalked out of the bedroom. He brushed past his wife without saying a word to her or giving her a glance, took his Stetson off the antler rack near the door, and left the house. Sam followed him to the shed behind the house, where he saddled his horse. He rode to the courthouse and dismounted, Sam following.

"I've got to tell my deputy where I'm going," Garber said.

"I'll go along," Sam said.

He followed Garber into the sheriff's office and stood near the door as Garber told his deputy what he was going to do. Sam wasn't sure what passed between them because Garber's back was to him and he couldn't hear what the sheriff said. The deputy shot a quick glance at Sam and immediately looked away again, nodding as he listened to the sheriff. Then Garber wheeled and strode past Sam.

As Garber mounted, Sam asked, "Have you talked to the people who were on the stage or to Zeke?"

"I don't know what you're talking about," Garber said. "I got in late last night and I was tired. I don't even know what happened."

"It wasn't what you expected," Sam said. "You figured Pa would be strung up or lying in the undertaker's parlor when you got back, but it didn't happen. Pa was taken off the stage near the top of Crow Hill."

"The hell he was," Garber said in amazement. "You know who done it?"

"I think it was Mike Hale," Sam said, "but I don't have the solid evidence you were talking about. That's why we're going out to see him."

They rode through town and started climbing Crow Hill. Presently Garber said, "I'm sorry I wasn't on the job, but I didn't look for anything like that to happen. I sure wasn't going to have to gun my friends down, so I left town, but I'm not as one-sided as you make out. I'm scared of Hale because he's a dangerous man, like I told you, but I don't like the bastard. He's a goddamn rustler and horse thief, and he gives the settlers a bad name because he poses as one of us, which he ain't, so I hope we can nail him."

"There's talk of declaring martial law in Bensen County," Sam said.

"Which is the last thing we want," Garber said. "Arresting and trying Mike Hale might prove we ain't as lawless as they claim we are."

Sam glanced at the sheriff, surprised at what seemed to be a turnaround in his attitude, but what he said made sense. Nobody on the homesteaders' side wanted martial law in Bensen County, and it was true that a show of law enforcement might put off talk of establishing it. It was also true that men like Mike Hale gave the settlers a bad name. Sam just hadn't given Garber credit for having enough sense to understand that, and he had assumed that the sheriff would take Hale's side, simply because Hale posed as a settler and was against the big cowmen.

Garber was staring straight ahead at the brow of the hill ahead of them, his mouth drawn tightly against his teeth. He was not a brave man, and he would have been the first to admit it. His estimate of Mike Hale was correct. The man was dangerous. Now Sam wondered how much help Garber would be in a pinch. Would he stand and fight if it came to that? Or would he turn tail and run and leave Sam to do the fighting? Well,

Sam told himself, there was no way to know until it happened. Besides, Sam had to admit he wasn't sure how brave he was in a real showdown. He'd find that out, too.

When they reached the crest of the hill, Sam reined up and dismounted. He said, "I don't know exactly where the stage was stopped, but it was somewhere south of here. There were two other passengers besides Pa in the coach. I've talked to them and I've talked to Zeke, but about all I learned was that three men stopped the stage. One of 'em looked like Hale. One of 'em was tall and slim, and one seemed to be a kid. The woman passenger said that the man who did the talking and shoved his gun barrel into the coach had a scar on the back of one hand. I hear Hale has a scar from a fight."

Garber nodded. "He does. I remember that. I'd guess the skinny fellow is named Marty Martin. The kid probably is his son Jerry. They're not wanted as far as I know, but they're like Hale, horse thieves and rustlers. I stopped at Hale's place for a drink a couple of months ago and they were there. They would have killed me if I'd made a wrong move. I was glad to get away alive."

Sam and Garber walked along the edge of the road, eyes on the steep bank to their left. Sam stopped and pointed into the ravine below the bank. "That's where they left their horses, looks like. Maybe yesterday afternoon just like Zeke and the others said."

He studied the soft dirt of the bank for a moment, then he added, "They slid down here. It's a safe bet that they held the stage up right here and took Pa down the back, then lit out. Think we can track 'em?"

Garber shook his head. "Not very far. There's a patch of hard pan east of here where we'll lose 'em."

"Then we might as well head straight for Hale's place," Sam said.

"Hale's no fool," Garber said. "He wouldn't hide your pa in his own shack."

"There's plenty of homesteader shacks and dugouts where he might hide Pa," Sam said. "We'll have to hunt for him."

"And that," Garber said, "is gonna be tough findin'."

Chapter 11

Sam and Ed Garber spent most of the day searching every dugout, soddy, and shack they had ever seen or heard about. Except for a few where the original homesteaders were still hanging on, they found no trace of life. Then, in late afternoon with the sun dipping down toward the Big Horns, Garber looked at Sam and swallowed.

"I know what you're going to say, Powers," the sheriff said, "and I don't like it one damn bit."

"You guessed right," Sam said. "We're paying Hale a visit."

"It's suicide," Garber said sourly. "If Martin and his kid are there, it'll be three guns against one, and they're tough hands. I ain't no such thing and I doubt like hell that you are."

Sam gave him a tight grin. "You know, Garber, I ain't real sure myself, but one good thing about this deal is it gives us a chance to find out. Otherwise we might die and never know."

Garber grumbled something again about it being suicide, but he turned south with Sam and didn't argue any more about it. They reached the canyon of the Dry Fork, dropped down into it, and followed it east. It was easier going than keeping north of the rim, where the country had been eroded by a series of parallel dry washes that created a great deal of slow up-and-down riding. As they passed a grove of cottonwoods, Sam pointed to the ground ahead of them.

"Somebody's ridden through here the last day or two," he said. "They mighta brought Pa this way."

Garber nodded. "That'd be a good guess. It's almost straight west of here where they took your pa off the stage, and the tracks are headed straight for Hale's place."

"Which means that Pa might be there," Sam said. "But I guess there's plenty of places on past Hale's outfit where they could have taken him."

Garber nodded somberly. "Like I said, I don't figger Hale's stupid enough to try to hide the old man at his place, but we won't know until we search it, and we don't have no warrant for that."

"I've got all the warrant I need." Sam patted the butt of his gun. "It's my show. Just keep 'em off my back."

Apparently Garber didn't hear what Sam said. He had reined up, his gaze on the north rim of the canyon. Sam turned his head to see what the sheriff was doing. When he saw that the law man had stopped, he pulled up, too, asking, "What's wrong?"

"Dunno." Garber touched up his horse with his spurs until he came alongside Sam. "I happened to look up there and saw somebody watching us. When he spotted me looking at him, he ducked back. Maybe I'm spooked, getting this close to Hale's hangout, but I saw enough of the fellow who was watching us to know that he looked a hell of a lot like the Martin kid."

They rode on, Sam thinking about what Garber had said. Sam shook his head. "I don't know that it means anything."

"Sure it does," Garber said. "If it was the Martin boy, it means Hale stationed him up there as a lookout. When we get out of this canyon, it's my guess we'll see the boy riding hell for leather to tell Hale we're coming."

"Why?"

Garber shrugged. "He wants to be warned if anybody comes through here." He paused and swallowed with an effort. "That might mean they're keeping your pa at Hale's place."

"We'll find out," Sam said.

He expected Garber to turn around and ride back to town, but the sheriff surprised him by continuing to ride beside him. He glanced at the lawman's face. Fear was there, all right. Sam wondered what his own face showed. His belly felt as if it was squeezed tightly against his backbone, and once more doubts plagued him. He was, he thought bitterly, a fool for risking his life and future for the stubborn old goat who had kicked him off the AP and promised to disinherit him. Then he shrugged. Fool or not, he could not turn back.

A mile farther on they rode out of the canyon, the sheer cliffs giving way to gentle slopes. From here they could see for miles across the grass. Sam realized immediately that Garber's guess had been accurate. A dustcloud rose ahead of them. The rider making it was hunched forward over his saddle horn, beating his horse with a quirt.

"You were dead right," Sam said. "Maybe it wasn't the Martin kid, but somebody's in a hurry to get to where he's going."

"That's a hell of a way to treat a horse," Garber said angrily. "If it was one of my men, I'd fire him for it."

"Maybe he's had his orders," Sam said.

Garber nodded. "Maybe he has at that. I don't figger Hale's a man to worry about how a horse is treated."

"No, I reckon not." Sam laughed shortly. "He can always steal another one. We knew damn well he was stealing both horses and cows from us when Pa was home, but we could never catch him at it."

They reached the Hale ranch half an hour later, if, Sam thought, it could be called a ranch. The house was a shack, obviously no more than one room, the barn was made of slabs, and on beyond it was a pole corral that held half a dozen horses. There was no sign of life about the place except for the horses. It was, Sam thought, the most dismal-looking layout he had ever seen.

They pulled up in front of the shack, Sam calling, "Hello the house."

The front door slammed open and Mike Hale strode out. He stopped and stared at Sam with the disdain of a man who felt superior to his visitor. His gaze swung to Garber, then back to Sam, his expression unchanged.

"This an official visit, Sheriff?" Hale asked, his gaze still pinned on Sam.

"Not exactly," Garber said uneasily.

"It ain't a social call," Sam said. "You heard about my Pa being taken off the stage?"

"Yeah, I heard he didn't get the hanging he deserved," Hale said sullenly. "What's that got to do with me?"

"We figure you're the bastard who took him," Sam said, "and we think you've got him hidden in your house or barn. We want to search 'em."

"The hell you will," Hale snapped. "Let's see your warrant, Sheriff."

"I don't have no warrant," Garber said, "but I can get one, and if I do, I'll be back with a posse of twenty men and blow you out of that shack you call a house if you get stubborn about it."

"You'll never get a posse of twenty men to come after me," Hale said. "I'm on your side, remember, and I was on your side when old man Powers and his killers rode into Bensen County. If you've forgotten, you'll soon remember when you try to put a posse together, because everybody else remembers. Likewise they remember it was my brother that Powers helped murder. Now get out of here before I give the signal that'll get you both killed."

"If you don't have Pa," Sam said, "why do you object to having your house and barn searched?"

"Because I've got a citizen's rights the same as the next man," Hale said. "I ain't no Philadelphia lawyer,

72

but I know a man's house is his castle, and you or nobody else has a right to search it without a warrant."

He stepped back so he was standing between Sam and Garber on one side, and the house on the other. He said ominously, "Two of my friends are inside. They've had their guns on you from the minute you rode in. Now if you ain't on your way in ten seconds, I'll give 'em the go ahead to blow you out of your saddles. The Martin kid is plumb hungry to get his first man, and you'd be as good as any."

"We're going," Garber said.

It would be suicide to stay, Sam told himself. He didn't doubt the truth of what Hale said about the two men in the house. He turned his horse and rode after Garber. Neither spoke until the men had topped the ridge north of Hale's shack and were out of his sight. Then Garber said, "You know something, Powers? He would have done it, and the chances are good that nobody else in the county would ever know what happened to us. There's plenty of country out here to bury us in."

"I figured that way, too," Sam said as he reined up and stepped down.

Garber rode on for another twenty feet, then stopped and looked back at Sam. "What kind of hairbrained scheme have you hatched up now?" he demanded.

"I ain't leaving here till we have a look around Hale's place," Sam said. "It don't stack up right to me, seeing how it would have been easier for him to have let us look in the house and barn. If we didn't find Pa, we'd have ridden on and that would have been the end of it."

Garber shook his head. "You don't savvy that son of a bitch. He's mean, but he's proud. It's a matter of principle with him. I don't think he'd have let us go inside if I'd had a warrant."

"Maybe," Sam admitted grudgingly, "but I'm staying until I'm sure. Besides, it'll do my soul good to cut Hale down a notch or two."

"Now just how do you expect to do that?" Garber

demanded. "I told you before that he was a tough hand. You oughtta know that now, after what happened. He wanted to kill us, and he would have if we'd made a wrong move. I tell you you'll never get into his house."

"I'll do it," Sam said. "You go on back to town if you want to."

Garber swore and rode on north. After going fifty yards, he turned his horse and came back. "Hell, Powers, I don't know why I listen to you, but I'd like a look into that house myself, even though I don't think the old man's there. How do you aim to work it?"

Sam glanced up at the sun, which was low over the Big Horns. He said, "It'll be dark in another couple of hours. Sooner or later they're going to have to come out of the house to take a leak if nothing else. When one of 'em does, I'll get him." He took off his hat and scratched his head. "I need you to keep two of 'em off my back while I handle one. We'll have to have some luck, but I think we can do it. I ain't so sure I can handle 'em alone."

Garber groaned. "Damned if you ain't bound to make a hero out of me. I ain't much for dying from an overdose of bravery, but I'll take a hand in your game."

"I guess I've been wrong about you," Sam said as the sheriff stepped down.

"No, you ain't been wrong," Garber said. "I know I ain't much of a credit to my office. The trouble is I know who elected me. I figured I owed 'em a good job of looking after their interest, just like the sheriff before me looked after your pa's interest and the others like him." He jerked a thumb toward Hale's shack. "If anybody brings martial law on Bensen County, it'll be men like him. He ain't really on our side, no matter what he says, though I reckon folks think he is." He sucked in a long breath and shook his head. "By God, I'd like to put him in the jug."

"This ought to be your chance," Sam said.

Garber nodded agreement. "That's why I'm backing your play."

They waited until the darkness was complete. A cloud cover had moved across the sky from the Big Horns, blotting out the light from the stars and the crescent moon. They mounted and rode south toward the shack. Sam had spent most of the last two hours on his belly at the top of the ridge, watching the shack to see if anyone left. He had remained there until it became too dark to see the buildings. If anyone had left, it had been within the last half hour.

When they were within fifty yards of the shack, they dismounted and, leaving their horses ground-hitched, eased forward, moving slowly and carefully so they would not give their presence away. They reached the shack and moved along the wall until they came to the corner of the building. There they waited, each minute seeming to drag out into an eternity.

The door of the shack was shut, but the window beside the door in the front wall showed that a lamp inside was lighted. Now and then Sam could hear a man laugh and the hum of conversation, but he could not make out any of the words.

He lost all sense of time, but it must have been more than an hour later when the front door slammed open and Hale stepped out, unbuttoning his pants as he moved across the hard, trodden earth of the yard, until he was out of the panel of light that fell through the open doorway and window.

Sam put a hand on Garber's arm, whispered, "Now," and, drawing his gun, took five long steps to reach Hale's back. He brought the gun barrel down in a vicious blow that took the starch out of Hale's legs and dropped him at Sam's feet. Quickly he dragged Hale's motionless body around the corner of the shack to where Garber stood. He had made no sound other than the crack of the gun barrel on Hale's skull. The Martin boy must have heard it and, not knowing what it was, moved to the door, calling, "Mike, what happened?"

When he received no answer, he stepped outside and stood there uncertainly, glancing around as he peered into the darkness. He moved farther away from the front door and raised his voice, "Mike?"

He turned his back to Sam, still twisting his head back and forth as he called once, "Damn it, Mike, answer me." It was, Sam thought, the best chance he would have. He plunged forward just as the boy turned and saw him. He tried to wheel away as he got off a frantic shout. "Pa!" Sam caught him on the side of the head with the gun barrel. It wasn't a knockout blow, but it put him on the ground.

Martin picked up a rifle and ran outside, but by the time he had cleared the doorway, Sam was sitting astride the boy, the muzzle of his gun digging into young Martin's belly.

"Drop your Winchester," Sam yelled, "if you don't want the kid to get a slug in his guts."

Martin hesitated, his rifle on the ready, as he peered at Sam and his boy, who were barely visible in the fringe of lamplight. Sam shouted, "In case you can't see us, I'm sitting on the kid and my gun's prodding him in the guts. If I drop my hammer, he's dead, and no matter how dead you shoot me, he'll get a dose of lead poisoning, so toss your Winchester out here where I can see it."

Martin obeyed, cursing loudly and with a variety of words. "Shut up," Sam snapped at him. "Get out here into the yard where I can see you. Sheriff, drag Hale over here so you can watch all three of 'em."

Martin moved forward as Garber dragged Hale's inert body back around the corner of the shack until he was lying beside the Martin boy. "All right," Sam said. "Watch 'em while I look in the house."

Garber drew his gun and lined it on Martin. The boy started to sit up, but lay back again when Garber kicked him in the ribs. He said, "Go ahead, Powers. I think they're gonna be good boys from now on."

Sam ran into the shack, expecting to find his father tied up and lying on the floor, but there was no one in the shack and no place to hide him. It was, as he had thought, a one-room house without even a closet or a pantry. Disappointed, he picked up a lantern and lit it, wondering how anyone could live in this filth. The smell was nauseating. A pile of dirty dishes was stacked on the table. A couple of frying pans were on the stove, each still partly filled with fried food left from supper. The only other furniture was the bunks and chairs.

Sam ran outside, calling, "I'm going into the barn. Pa ain't here."

The barn was just as empty as the house. There were six stalls for horses and a haymow in front of the mangers. Nothing else. No place where a man could be hidden. He ran back to the house. "Let's ride," he said as he set the lantern down. He picked up Martin's rifle and threw it as far as he could into the darkness, then yanked Hale's and the boy's hand guns from their holsters and threw them after the rifle.

Hale was sitting up now and staring at Garber's gun. He said hoarsely, "I'll get you bastards for this and don't you forget it."

Garber backed away, calling, "Stand pat, all three of you."

Sam had disappeared around the corner of the shack, but Garber paused before he cleared the corner, his gun still in his hand. The kid jumped up, but when Garber fired, putting a bullet into the dirt a foot in front of him, the boy dived back down and lay motionless.

Garber ran after Sam, hoping the three men could not tell whether he had gone or was still watching them. He reached the horses a moment after Sam did. Mounting, they rode north, pausing once to listen, but there was no sound of pursuit.

"Looks like we wasted our time," Garber said.

"No," Sam said. "At least we know Pa's not there."

"But you don't know if he's alive or not," Garber said, "and you can be damned sure that Hale will keep his word. He'll try to get back at us some way or another, maybe plug us from ambush when we ain't looking."

"We've got to go on the idea Pa's still alive," Sam said, "until we know otherwise. As for them drygulching us, we'll just have to keep our eyes peeled. I think he'll finish up his business with Pa before he tackles either one of us. When he does, he'll likely come after me first."

"What are you gonna do now?"

"Go home and sleep what's left of the night."

"Then what?"

"Wait for Hale to make a move," Sam answered. "If he's got Pa, like we think, he'll make one in a hurry after what happened tonight." He paused, then added, "No, we didn't waste our time at all. We proved we were pretty tough hands ourselves."

"Yeah," Garber said with pride. "By God, we did."

Chapter 12

Tony Arbanz sat at his desk most of the morning, trying to concentrate on the lead story he had to compose before the *Sentinel* went to press, and completely failing. He had to tell his readers as much as he knew about what had happened yesterday, omitting, of course, his part in the lynching scheme, but all he could think of was Julie Larkin and the hour he had spent in bed with her that morning.

He had always been fascinated by the question of fate, of good and bad luck. He had never understood the why of it, although he had an intuitive feeling that there was no such thing as an accident. The odds of a man finding a reputable publisher like Stafford and Buel and a beautiful woman to go to bed with all on the same morning were more than he cared to contemplate, but certainly far beyond logic.

And Julie Larkin was both beautiful and sensual. He'd had his share of women over the years, but none could compare with Julie. When they had finished, she had held him in her arms and kissed him, and said, "Oh, Tony, no woman could ever hope to have a better lover than you. Now I know why I came to Crow City." Those words, more than the actual act of mating, had lifted him into a state of euphoria that still gripped him.

His mind kept going back to that hour and those words until he finally gave up, rose from his desk, and began pacing the floor. He was a disciplined man, and now he was angry with himself for wasting time by dreaming when there was work to be done. Still, he asked himself how a man could think of anything as mundane as a news story after experiencing Julie Larkin, and he had indeed experienced her as he had never known another woman.

He crossed the street at noon and had dinner in the hotel dining room, hoping he would see Julie again, but she did not appear. By the time he returned to his print shop, he had come back down to earth, and for the first time he began to question his good fortune.

In many ways Tony Arbanz was a dreamer and an idealist, but still he was a practical man, and he was very much aware that the mathematical odds of meeting an editor who just happened to be in Crow City and was interested in publishing his manuscript were a million to one. To compound the odds, the chance of that woman falling in love with him at first sight would jack up the odds to a billion to one. The thought had been in his mind that morning, but now it nagged him with a depressing sense of certainty.

He finally got his thoughts back on the track enough to compose his news story, but now the dark clouds of doubt gathered in his mind. Julie had to be playing some kind of game, but what? He could not even hazard a guess.

The questions finally boiled down in his mind to one. Who and what was Julie Larkin? She was not a whore. She was an educated and self-assured woman of grace and charm. He knew whores. Perhaps there were good ones with hearts of gold according to tradition, but he had never known one. Julie simply did not have the brand on her.

He tried to put her out of his mind and think about Betty and Sam, and how his life would be without Betty. He didn't like the prospect, but he told himself he'd had no choice last night, and he was glad they had come to an agreement of sorts. At least he did not have to continue the charade of threatening to kill Sam if he came around the house to see Betty. He knew that she was relieved, too. He had never really intended to harm Sam in any way, and he had been worried that he might be shoved into a corner where he would have to make his threat good.

Sam had been dead right when he'd said that the only thing Arbanz had against him was the fact that Adam Powers was his father. This line of thinking brought old man Powers back into his consciousness, and he was filled once more with the old driving hatred that had grown in him from the moment he had been thrown out of the Cheyenne Club, until it had become a fever in his blood. It had only temporarily abated when Sam had convinced him that Adam had actually been kidnapped by a third party.

If Adam was dead, then he was out of Arbanz's reach and there was nothing he could do to him. But suppose his first suspicion had been right—that Sam had somehow planned and carried out the abduction, that Adam right now was out there on the AP in the best of health and laughing up his sleeve because he had outwitted the credulous fools in Crow City who had planned his execution?

He had to know for sure, but this was more than he could accomplish singlehanded. He rose and left the print shop, locking the door behind him, and strode down the street to the bank. He went in, nodding at the teller who was working on a ledger at a desk near the wall.

"Jason in?" Arbanz asked.

The teller jerked a thumb toward the back room. "He's in his office."

Arbanz pushed aside the swinging gate at the end of the counter, stepped through it, and crossed to Jason Small's private office. He tapped on the door, heard Small say to come in, and opened the door. The banker was leaning back in his swivel chair, an oversized cigar tucked into one corner of his mouth. It always struck Arbanz as being strange that Small, who was small by size as well as by name, would let himself be dwarfed by a mere cigar.

The banker nodded when he saw who his visitor was. He motioned to a chair as he said, "I'm glad to see you, Tony. I was bored sitting here and thinking how I had earned my salary for the day just by mentally picturing my interest, which is piling up a little every day. It's a great feeling to know that each day makes me a little richer, even if I don't turn a hand."

"You're a wit," Arbanz said sourly. "You should write a column for the *Sentinel*."

"You're in an ugly mood," Small said reprovingly. "What's the matter with the scene I just drew?"

"It's not practical," Arbanz said. "It depends on how much water there is for irrigation this summer, whether we get any hail or an early frost in the fall, and if prices are up enough for the farmers to make a profit."

"Oh hell." Small grimaced, his thin lips tightening around his cigar. "You're sure a ray of sunshine. What are you here for, just to worry me? Or maybe ask me to renew your loan?"

Arbanz shook his head. "I'll have my interest on time. In fact, I have a venture brewing that may make me a rich man. If it develops as I expect, I'll be able to repay my loan. No, I'm having second thoughts about old man Powers. Sam came to see me last night and talked me into believing that the old bastard had really been kidnapped, but I got to thinking about it and it struck me that Sam was lying. Chances are the old son of a bitch is out there right now sitting in his living room giving us the horse laugh."

Small shrugged. "Let him stay there if that's the case."

"No, by God," Arbanz shouted. "We can't let him outsmart us. If he's still alive, he needs his neck stretched as much as he ever did."

The banker took the cigar out of his mouth and turned it slowly between his forefingers as he studied it. He said slowly, "Tony, you're possessed by your hatred of Powers. If he had showed up here in town, I'd have helped put the rope around his neck, but he didn't. Now I say let sleeping dogs lie."

Arbanz stared at him in disbelief. "You've always been the real leader in this county, Jason. You were the leader when the invaders came, and you were the man who organized us and planned for the hanging. What in hell has got into you now?"

"Nothing has changed the way I feel about Adam Powers," Small said, "but I've retained enough of my sanity to know that we've lost our chance. We'll never get the homesteaders worked up again enough to hang him, so we've got to forget it. If two or three of us do the job, we'll be arrested for murder. If we could have done it the minute he stepped off the stage with practically every man in the county having a hand in it, we wouldn't have been touched."

For a moment Arbanz sat with his hands on his knees, staring at the banker. He said, "Jason, I tell you we've got to go out to the AP and see if he's there. Four or five of us could do it. If we mask our faces, nobody will know who we are."

Small rose, put the cigar back into his mouth, and fired it. He said, "Looks like I've wasted my time talking to you. You didn't hear a word I said. Now you go on back to your newspaper and let me go on dreaming about how my interest is piling up."

Small walked to the door, opened it, and stood waiting for Arbanz to leave. Arbanz rose, then hesitated, staring at the banker's set face. He finally realized there was nothing he could do but get out, that there were no words he could say that would change the banker's mind. He stalked out of the office, across the lobby to the door, and out into the afternoon sunshine.

He was so driven by his hatred of Adam Powers and his hunger to see the man swing that he turned without conscious thought toward Fred Ames's store. When he stepped inside, he was temporarily blinded by the gloom of the interior of the long room, which had no windows except the ones facing the street.

"Why, good afternoon, Tony," Mrs. Ames said. "I bet you want to see Fred."

He saw her then, standing behind the counter on the grocery side of the room. She was stacking cans of fruit on a shelf. She was a small, tight-lipped woman who had the reputation of leading Fred around by the nose, but Arbanz had always found her courteous and had felt she did not deserve what was said about her.

"That's right," Arbanz said, "but I don't see him."

"Oh, he's in the back room moving the sugar," she said, laughing. "He's worse than a woman with her furniture. He's always moving something."

"I'll go interrupt his work," Arbanz said, and strode along the counter to the door that opened into the storeroom.

Ames was in the back lifting a sack of sugar. Arbanz watched him carry it to a pile he was building along the west wall. Arbanz called, "Fred, is that what you'd call busy work?"

Ames turned, saw who it was, and sat down on the pile where he had just deposited the sack he had been carrying. "I reckon Nan would call it that," he said as he drew a plug of tobacco from a pocket. "She's always joshing me about the way I move stuff around, but I have a reason for doing what I do. It's just that she don't savvy the reason."

Ames laughed. If the occasion had been different, Arbanz would have laughed, too. The storekeeper had a talent for laughing at himself, a talent Arbanz realized that he himself did not have, and he envied the man for it. He crossed the room, upended an empty box, and sat down on it.

"Fred, I'm here to get some help," he said. "I've been thinking that old man Powers just plain outsmarted us. Or Sam did. I'm not sure which one did it, or how it was done, but the more I think about it, the more I'm convinced that he's out there right now on the AP laughing his head off at the way we got left high and dry."

"That so?" Ames chewed for a moment, then spat in the direction of a spittoon, one of half a dozen that were scattered around the storeroom. "Then I reckon he fooled us."

"I don't know for sure," Arbanz said, "but I think we ought to get some men together and ride out there tonight and search the place. If he is there, we'll bring him to town and do the job we figured on doing."

Ames continued to chew for a time, then he said, "You talked to Jason?"

"Yes," Arbanz said, "but I'm sorry to say he doesn't see it the way I do."

"That's what I figured," Ames said. "Well, Tony, you're a hothead and Jason ain't. I ain't, neither. I guess we needed a man like you to keep us stirred up. If we could have strung the old bastard up when he got off the stage, I'd have said it was a good job we done, but he wasn't on the stage. If we go out there now, somebody's going to get killed." He shook his head. "No, Tony, I figure we'd better let things ride for a while. I ain't sure the old devil will ever show his face in town. If he does . . ." Ames shrugged. "Well then, I might change my mind."

For a long moment Arbanz didn't speak. He had expected this reaction, but now that he had it, he was angry, too angry to speak for a moment. Fred Ames was good-natured, but he was also stubborn. Arbanz knew very well that if he couldn't change Jason Small's mind, he couldn't change Fred Ames's.

The fact that Ames had called him a hothead irritated him. He hadn't dreamed that anyone in Bensen County thought of him that way. He had fancied himself a community leader, a man calling attention to a vital need, a man helping correct a gross miscarriage of justice. Now to be called a hothead . . . to realize that he was alone in his hunger to bring about what he thought of as simple justice, was too much. He realized he had better not say anything.

He rose as he said sharply, "All right, Fred."

He stomped out of the room, ignoring Ames's words, "I've got a bottle cached away out here, Tony."

He went on, pretending he didn't hear Mrs. Ames say, "You didn't stay long."

Outside he turned toward his print shop, feeling completely alone in a town that a few hours before he had considered his home, a friendly town where he had been welcomed and where he had expected to live out the last years of his life.

Then he thought about Betty, who was leaving him and his home to marry Sam Powers, Adam Powers's son, and the sense of injustice and ingratitude grew in him until it had wiped out the last trace of the euphoria he'd had that morning. He thought bitterly that in all of his life he'd never experienced a day that had begun so well and had turned out so miserably.

By the time he reached his print shop, Arbanz told himself that when a man lost the support of two friends he had counted on, when he couldn't get them to listen to his argument with open minds, it was time to sack his saddle.

He unlocked his front door and went in, and then, with the familiar smell of printer's ink and paper in his nostrils, the sight of the untidy shop with its battered desk and tables and type stand, the sense of defeat was stripped from him. His mind suddenly made a complete turnaround that was characteristic of him. He had his newspaper, and in his skilled hands it would be a lethal weapon to destroy Adam Powers.

By God, he told himself, he wasn't finished. Not by a long shot.

Chapter 13

Adam Powers had undergone many trials in his long and lusty life. Some had been painful, some merely irritating, but none had made him suffer like this. Being held in a cave dug out of the side of a cliff with its stink and foul air and perpetual darkness was nothing less than hell.

At times Adam knew he hallucinated. He saw things that he knew weren't really there, strange monsters that occupied the black corners or slithered around the room and crawled across his bunk. Sometimes he screamed in terror; then the sound of a shrill voice that he recognized as his own brought him out of it. He would lie there then, shaking and sweating, and wishing for death.

He had never been a man to seek death, at least consciously, although when he was rational and looked back on the past year, he realized he would have welcomed it. Now, plagued by the wisdom of hindsight, he could see that Sam had been right when he had argued with him about riding off to join the invaders. It could have ended only one way, the way it had ended, and the chances were that if Hale had not taken him off the stage, he would have died in Crow City.

He was hungry, but when he lit a candle and built a fire and cooked a meal, he could not eat it. He would sit at the table staring at the plate of bacon and beans, and end up drinking a cup of coffee, then blowing out the candle and feeling his way back to the bunk.

The darkness was the worst of all. The hours dragged by in monotonous sameness without Adam knowing when it was day or when it was night. Sometimes he could see the thin line of light around the door, but then he wasn't sure whether it was sunlight or moonlight. The sun had always regulated his life. When the AP was at its height of size and power, he had gotten up with the sun or before it rose, and he had seen to it that everyone else on the ranch did the same.

More often than not, he had eaten breakfast with Ida by lamplight in the kitchen of the big house, while the men were eating in the cook shack. Within the hour he'd be in the saddle with the crew, starting the day.

Now he was lost because there was no sun to regulate his day. One hour was like another. He didn't know whether he had been here one day or a week. Sometimes he had heard people ride by and had sat up and yelled, but no one had heard. He was losing his strength, but he didn't care. He told himself over and over that he wanted to die. It was like a refrain without words, but always with the same tune.

He had never thought much about God, but now he talked to Him and asked Him to take his life. But still he lived in a dark and oppressive world, and for the first time in his life he felt regret about many things he had done, about the way he had treated people, even about his attitudes and goals in life. It all could have been so different, and he told himself that this, too, was hell. He wondered if he had already died and didn't know it.

He did not regret the way he had fought to keep the AP or the way he felt about the homesteaders. They were thieves who took land that belonged to him by right if not by law, cowardly men who had moved into a country after it had been tamed and made safe for people like them. What he had done was right and his convictions on the matter were right, and he would do the same things over again if given the opportunity. If he ever had to stand before an Almighty God and defend his actions and convictions, he would do it.

No, his regrets were in a different area. He thought about the way he had been raised, his parents and his brothers, and how he had been rebellious at home, defying them and finally running away from home when he was fifteen. He had been the oldest in his family, and he had used his strength to bully and sometimes abuse his brothers.

It had been a long time since he had even thought about his childhood, but now the memories flowed back. He was reminded of the old saying about how a man's life flashes through his mind in a matter of seconds when he is drowning. That was happening now, except it lasted for hours, not seconds. He could not blot those memories out of his consciousness. He thought of events he had not thought about for years; he wondered what had happened to his parents and his brothers, and he was ashamed that he had never written home.

The West had swallowed him, just as it had swallowed many restless boys, and now he realized how his mother must have wondered and worried about him, but she had probably died not knowing whether he was alive or dead.

She and his father must have died by now. If not, they would be old and helpless, perhaps living in a poverty he could have alleviated. Not now, because he was broke, but there had been a time when he had had all the money a man could use, and he could have done something for them.

He thought of Ida and what a good wife she had been, but he had never told her. He had taken her for granted. In a way he had abused her. Not physically, but by neglect and by being too demanding. It was a sorry situation, he told himself, that this knowledge came to him now when it was too late. He had begun to be aware of this when he had been held a prisoner in Cheyenne, and if he could have gone home the day he was taken off the stage, he might have told her some of the things he should have said to her twenty years ago.

It was the same with Sam. He remembered the night Sam was born and how proud he had been to have a son and how he had wanted more. Then when he had learned he would have no more children, he blamed Ida for it. The fact that it was not her fault had nothing to do with the way he felt. He had always been a man to blame someone else, and Ida had to be the one.

He had blamed Sam, too, for being too independent, for being rebellious, for actually defying him at times. Now he realized that he had been much the same kind of boy. The difference had been that Sam had swallowed his pride and had stayed home, accepting a responsibility that he, Adam, had never even known he had.

Suddenly he was crying, crying tears of regret for lost time and lost opportunities, something he had never thought he would do. He was a broken and beaten man, and that hurt, too. Funny, he thought, damned funny that he could see so many things in their right relationship that he had never dreamed about in the days of normal living. He was a different man; he had been reborn, but it was too goddamned late.

Suddenly the door was opened and the harsh sunlight streamed into the dugout. Mike Hale stood in the doorway, a blocky, formidable figure.

Adam sat up and rubbed his eyes, uncertain about whether Hale was real, or something his twisted mind had manufactured, like the monsters that had inhabited the darkness. He decided Hale was real, the sunlight was real, the fresh air that flowed in through the doorway was real. He stood up, swayed, and sat down again, not sure he could remain upright.

"How are you getting along, old man?" Hale asked

as he came into the dugout and sat down at a table.

"How do you expect me to get along?" Adam asked bitterly. "I don't know what day it is. I don't even know how long you've had me locked up in here."

"A day or two," Hale said, grinning.

"You son of a bitch." Adam rose, swaying again, but only for a moment, and walked slowly to the door.

"You try making a run for it, and you'll get a slug in the back," Hale said. "I ain't of a mind to run you down, and you're just as valuable to me dead as alive."

"I'm worth nothing to you," Adam said.

"Oh, yes, you are," Hale said. "That's why I came by. How much do you figure Sam will pay me to send you back?"

"Pay?" Adam turned to stare at Hale. "Why, he wouldn't pay you a cent."

"I figure he will," Hale said. "The damned fool showed up at my place last night and wanted to search my buildings. He figured I was hiding you in my house or barn. I don't know what kind of a jackass he thinks I am. He had the sheriff with him, but they didn't have no warrant, so I wouldn't let 'em do it.

"I figured they'd gone on home, but by God, they waited till after dark, got the drop on me, and knocked me cold. When I came out of it, I was lying on the ground with a man-sized headache and they had their guns on the Martins. Sam hunted around and didn't find nothing. Before they rode off, I told him I'd get him for it and I will."

Adam continued to stare at Hale, his numbed mind having trouble grasping what the man had said. The fact that his son had thought enough of him after all that had happened to risk his life in an effort to rescue him was more than he could believe. And for Ed Garber, a homesteader sheriff, to give Sam a hand was even more unbelievable.

Adam put a hand to his forehead, trying to think. Hale was holding him for ransom. That notion had never really occurred to him before. Adam knew Sam had no money and he knew that the AP wasn't worth much, but apparently Hale didn't know. For the first time since he had been locked up in the dugout, Adam had a slim hope that he'd come out of this alive.

"Well?" Hale said impatiently. "I'm paying a visit to the AP tonight and I'm tossing a rock through a window with a message for Sam. I've got to have some idea how much to ask for."

Adam shook his head. "You're barking up the wrong tree. What you've forgotten is that rustlers like you robbed me blind for years. I didn't have no money when I left and Sam wouldn't have no way to make any while I was gone."

"Hogwash," Hale snapped. "This is my last job around here. I'm pulling out in a few days and I aim to make a little dinero before I go. Now I'm asking you once more. How much do you figure Sam can raise?"

"Nothing, I told you," Adam said. "Anyhow, why should Sam pay you anything? You're going to kill me before you leave, ain't you?"

"Sure, but Sam don't know that." Hale grinned. "I didn't take you for the money, though. You're here because you killed my brother, and I sure as hell wish that Seth Alexander and the rest of 'em was here with you. They ain't, but I've got you, so I might as well make something out of it. Now you'd better answer my question. How much can Sam raise? $10,000?"

Adam rubbed his forehead, trying to think of something to say that made sense. Hale might kill him today. It didn't make much difference whether he did it today or tomorrow or the day after, as far as Hale was concerned, but the longer he could stall the outlaw, the more chance he had at being rescued.

"The only thing he can do," Adam said slowly, "is to go to the bank and mortgage the AP. If he does, he'll need my signature. It's something I've always told him we'd never do, but he might try it anyway. But hell, you know Fred Ames. I don't have no idea how much Fred would loan him, but it sure wouldn't be over $5,000."

Hale cursed. "Chicken feed," he said scornfully, "but you might be giving it to me straight. Old Fred is too tight to loan him very much." He took a folded piece of paper and a stubby pencil from his pocket. "Come here. You're writing a letter to Sam."

Adam turned and looked out into the sunlight, at the brush, at the grove of cottonwoods, at the canyon wall that rose south of the stream bed, and he wondered if the Martin kid was still on the north rim hungering for his first kill. He turned slowly and walked to the table, thankful for this last look at a world that was lighted by the sun. He had thought he would never see that world again.

He sat down at the table and Hale pushed the paper and pencil toward him. "Don't need much," he said. "Just enough to give Sam the idea. I guess he knows your handwriting?"

"He knows it, all right," Adam said.

"Just say 'pay it' and sign your name," Hale ordered. "That'll be enough."

Adam picked up the pencil and moistened the lead on the tip of his tongue. He hesitated, wishing he could think of something to add that would give Sam a clue as to where he was being held, but he could not. He scrawled "Pay it," and signed his name as Hale had directed. He was shocked by how quavery his handwriting was, but it was legible. Hale picked up the paper, glanced at it and, folding it, slipped it into his shirt pocket.

"There's a lot of ways of dying, old man," Hale said, "but since you're playing along with me, I'll make it easier than I intended." He walked to the door, then stopped and looked back, a thumb coming up to shove his hat back on his head. He asked, "How many bullet holes did you bastards put into Lon before he died?"

Adam didn't answer. He stared past Hale at the sunlight, the brush, the cottonwoods, the canyon wall beyond the trees, and for the first time in his life he saw beauty in a simple scene that was no different from scenes he had looked at millions of times. But he had never really seen them then. It was a lesson, he thought sadly, that many men never learn, and it was too late for him.

Hale laughed. "You just think about how many bullet holes Lon had in him and you can ask yourself how many you deserve."

Hale went out and closed the door. Adam was in darkness again, but for the first time in hours his mind was clear. He had not lost his sanity as he had told himself so many times he had. All he could think of was the risk that Sam had taken to free him. If he never left this dugout alive, at least he was glad he knew what Sam had tried to do.

Chapter 14

Sam had hoped to sleep late the morning after he returned from his search for Adam, but habit was too strong. He woke shortly after sunup. For a time he lay in bed trying to think of shacks and dugouts that he and Garber might have missed, or even of a cave where Hale could be holding his father. The old man had to be someplace out there, someplace that would hide him.

The thought occurred to him again that Hale might have murdered his father and buried him someplace on the prairie or at the bottom of a ravine. If that had happened, he would never find the body. No, he couldn't accept that. Not yet. Hale was not a man to miss the chance of making a few dollars, and he was smart enough to know that Sam would demand some evidence that would prove Adam was alive.

Sam heard his mother getting breakfast in the kitchen. He stretched and yawned, dead tired, but he realized that his feeling probably stemmed more from frustration than physical fatigue. He simply didn't know what to do until Hale made his proposition, It would, he hoped, come today.

He went downstairs to the kitchen, nodding at his mother and Bronc Collins, who was sitting at the table drinking a cup of coffee. He pumped a basin of water, washed, and combed his hair, ignoring his mother, who was standing beside the stove watching him, one hand on the coffee pot.

"Well?" Ida Powers asked, a hint of impatience in her voice. "Did you find him?"

"If I had, he'd be here," Sam said irritably, then threw up his hands. "I'm sorry, Ma. I'm whipped. We rode most of the day looking for him, then had a run-in with Hale and his two men, and rode most of the night getting home. We looked in every shack and dugout we could find and we didn't turn up anything. He's just gone."

As Sam sat down at the table, Bronc asked, "Did I hear you say we?"

"That's what I said." Sam nodded. "Ed Garber helped me, and it was a good thing he did or I woulda been in trouble at Hale's place."

"Now that don't make no sense at all." Bronc shook his head. "Garber helping you look for Adam? No sir, not one damned bit."

Sam grinned. "Well, it took a little persuading at first to get him started, but once he figured out it would be a good thing for him and the rest of the homesteaders to put Hale in the jug, he done all right."

Ida poured Sam's coffee and brought him a platter of flapjacks and bacon. "I guess it goes to prove that there's some good in everybody, though I always thought you'd have to look twice to find it in Ed Garber."

She didn't say anything more until Sam had finished eating. Then she asked, "What are you going to do now?"

"I wish I could think of something," he said. "We could make a wider swing. There's a hundred places in the county we ain't looked, but we both figured Hale would be holding Pa tolerably close to his place, so I don't think there's any use doing that. We've got to wait till we hear from him."

"How much do you think he'll ask for?" Ida said.

"I don't have no idea," Sam answered, "but I know we don't have it, no matter what he wants. I thought I'd ride into town and talk to Fred Ames. It would help if we knew what he'd loan us."

"He won't loan you nothing," Bronc said. "The spread belongs to Adam. You can't mortgage it without his signature. I don't figure Ames would loan you anything nohow, feeling about Adam the way he does."

"I know you're right," Sam agreed, "but I've got to ask. We don't have no other place to go. Even if we rounded up every head we've got and sold 'em, we wouldn't have as much as he'll ask. Besides, it'd take time, and Hale will probably give us about twenty-four hours."

As he rose, Bronc asked, "Anything you want me to do?"

"Stick close to the house and keep your gun on all day," Sam said. "It ain't likely he'll do anything crazy, but he said he'd get me for what I done to him last night, and I'm damned sure he'll try something sooner or later."

He went out into the clear morning air that held a bite even at this time of year. He saddled up and rode to the Arbanz place, wanting to warn Betty. Hale knew they were engaged, and he would not be above harming her to get at Sam. She saw him coming and ran out of the house as he dismounted. He held out his arms to her and she literally fell into them, clutching him with a passionate grip that was unusual for her.

"I'm glad you stopped," she said, her face pressed hard against his shirt. "I don't know what's going on and I don't like it."

He put both hands on the top of her head and forced it back so he could see her face. "I don't like what's going on, either, but I don't reckon I'm thinking about the same thing you are."

"Oh, you don't know what I'm talking about, do you?" she said. "I'm sorry. I've never mentioned Daddy's book to you because he asked me not to talk about it to anyone. Ever since he came here, he's been working on a book telling all he knows about the invasion and the attitudes and feelings of the men who planned it, mostly Adam and Seth Alexander. He's almost done with it. Just a chapter, I think, to write yet.

"Well, that woman who was on the stage, Larkin I think her name is, claims she's an editor and she wants to buy the book. You know how Daddy gets when he's excited. He loses his common sense and believes what he wants to believe, but I don't. I just don't believe she's being honest, but he won't listen to me."

"You think it's some kind of a con game?" Sam asked.

"I don't know," she answered. "I know Daddy doesn't have any money, but she may think he has." She shook her head. "Sam, it seems too much to have this happen, just to have it fall in his lap. Daddy came home last night and worked on that book till two o'clock trying to finish it so she can read the last chapter."

Sam thought about it a moment, then he said, "I don't know anything about the book business. Probably not as much as you do, but it strikes me that this is a phony deal. The invasion is important to us, but I doubt like hell that it's important enough to get a publishing company excited about it."

She nodded. "That's what I told Daddy. A book like that would sell in Wyoming, or maybe all over the West, but it takes more of a market than that to make a book profitable for the publisher."

"You said Tony tells the part that Pa and Seth Alexander had in planning the invasion."

Sam paused, turning an idea over in his mind that had just occurred to him. There had to be some explanation for the Larkin woman pretending to be an editor who was excited about Arbanz's book, if she was pretending, and it seemed logical to assume that she was.

Finally he said, "You know, if Pa had the opportunity to keep a book like that from being published, he'd do it."

"So Alexander might be behind the Larkin woman," Betty said. "He has the opportunity. I hadn't thought of that, but maybe she is here to find some way to kill the book. Even to buy it and then see that it was never published."

"Maybe," Sam agreed. "The whole Wyoming Stock Association would be just as interested as Alexander in getting rid of the book."

"They raised enough money to finance the invasion," she said. "They could certainly raise enough to hire the Larkin woman to get something on Daddy so the book would never be published. Maybe she's hoping to blackmail him."

"Or kill him," Sam said. "I don't want to scare you, but Tony knows as much as anybody about how the invasion started. He can say they are murderers who should have been hung. He's said that in the *Sentinel* right along, but a book is different from a newspaper. Nobody reads the *Sentinel* outside of Bensen County, but the book might be read anywhere."

"The cattlemen have a lot of power in Washington," Betty said. "A book like that could hurt them back there." She turned from Sam and began pacing back and forth. "It's probably worse than I thought. I assumed she would offer him a phony contract, wanting him to advance some money to get it published. He'd think it was a proper contract and try to raise the money. Maybe borrow it from the bank."

"Either way I don't see what I can do," Sam said. "Or you, either. Tony wouldn't listen to either one of us. If she's really aiming to kill the book, about all she can do is to get hold of it and destroy it. Even if she did, he could write it again."

"If he's alive to do it," she said miserably. "I guess we'll just have to wait. Maybe she'll give herself away."

"I had my own reasons for stopping." Sam told her what he had done the day before, then added, "I'd feel better if you'd ride over to the AP and stay with Ma today. I told Bronc to stick close to the house. I don't have no idea what Hale will do, but he might come here. He's liable to do anything, and I sure don't want anything happening to you because of what I've done."

"It won't," she said. "I'll lock the house and stay inside. I've got a gun and I wouldn't hesitate to use it on Mike Hale."

"Ma would love to have you," he said.

"I'd love visiting with her, too," Betty said, "but I think I'm better off here until I know more about what's going on. Daddy might come home and want me."

"All right," he said, and reached for her.

She came into his arms and clutched him convulsively. "Oh, Sam," she whispered. "I'm scared. Too many things are happening."

"I know," he said. "I feel helpless and that's a feeling I'm not used to." He mounted, then looked down at her. "I'm headed for town, then I'm going home and wait. I don't know what else I can do. You stay inside. Promise?"

"I promise," she said.

He rode away, turning back once to wave. He realized that Betty was as worried about her father as he was about his, and it was possible that Tony

Arbanz was in as much danger as Adam Powers. Sam didn't know Seth Alexander well, but he knew the cowman well enough to be sure that he was as capable of murder as Mike Hale was if it served his purpose.

Sam was convinced that Adam had been a pawn in Alexander's hands, that the invasion had been Alexander's idea in the first place, and that Adam, bitter because of his losses, had gone along with the scheme without realizing what the results might be.

As far as Arbanz was concerned, he couldn't think of anything he could do except to go to the man and warn him to stay away from Julie Larkin. That would be the height of folly. It would be all that was needed to break the uneasy truce he had reached with Arbanz the night before. This was Betty's problem and he had to stay out of it.

Sam reached town and reined up in front of the bank. He stepped down and tied, pausing as his glance moved along one side of the nearly deserted Main Street and then the other. He was reminded of the day when he expected to see his father step off the stage, the day when it seemed that every homesteader in the county was in town, the day he had faced Tony Arbanz, Fred Ames, and Jason Small with every intention of killing them if they tried to carry out their threat to lynch Adam.

That day seemed a long time ago. Now he was about to ask Small for whatever amount of money it would take to save Adam's life. He had never attempted anything before in which he had been so certain of failure. The only reason he was attempting it now was there was no one else to turn to.

He pictured each businessman as his gaze completed the circle of the business block. They were all as antagonistic as Small and Ames except John Doyle, and Doyle never had any great amount of cash. A few hundred dollars maybe. No more. Business simply had not been good for him lately. If he did get ahead a little, he put his spare cash into his ranch.

Sam sucked in a long breath and entered the bank.

The teller looked at him and turned away. The man had come to town a few days after Small had started the bank. Apparently they had known each other before they came to Crow City. Sam suspected the teller had been hired because he made a point of agreeing with Small and not because he had any great talent for banking.

"I want to see Mr. Small," Sam said.

The teller pretended he didn't see or hear Sam. For just a moment Sam hesitated, then he slammed back the gate at the end of the counter and started toward Small's private office.

"Wait," the teller screamed. "I'll see if he has time to see you."

Sam stopped halfway between the gate and the open door of Small's office. The teller ran to be sure he kept ahead of Sam, went into the office, and closed the door. It was, Sam thought ruefully, typical of the way most of the Crow City people reacted to him. They didn't hate him the way they hated Adam and Seth Alexander and the others, and although they were usually more courteous than the teller, they were always suspicious of him.

The teller came out a minute later, leaving the door open. He said grudgingly, "Mr. Small will see you now."

Sam went into the office, wondering if Small would be as rude as the teller had been. He said, "Good morning, Jason."

"Good morning, Sam," Small said, motioning to a chair. "The situation is a little different than it was the last time we met."

"Yes, it is," Sam agreed as he dropped into the chair. "I don't know if you heard or not, but it seems like Mike Hale is the man that took Pa off the stage."

"No, I hadn't heard," Small said.

"I ain't had no word from him," Sam went on, "but I expect to get a ransom demand. You know we ain't done so well the last few years with the rustlers cleaning us out the way they have, so my mother and I don't have no money if we do hear from Hale."

"So?" Small said, his lips tightening around his cigar.

"I'm here to find out how much you would loan us if we hear from the kidnappers," Sam said.

"I thought you were leading up to that." Small took the cigar out of his mouth and leaned forward. "Sam, you know I won't loan you a damned nickel. In the first place, you need Adam's signature to give me a mortgage on the AP. In the second place, I don't care what happens to Adam. If it is Hale, he'll kill your pa because of what happened to his brother Lon, and in my opinion he would be justified in doing it."

"It would be murder," Sam said. "I didn't think you'd take to that. . . ."

"You don't think anything of the kind," Small snapped, jabbing his cigar at Sam. "I'm not much concerned about Lon Hale, but I'm not sure that Bud Larkin deserved what he got. What I am concerned about is what would have happened to me and Tony and Fred and the rest of us who live in Crow City.

"Shooting a known rustler like Lon Hale is one thing, but coming on to Crow City and hanging every businessman and county official they could get their hands on is something else. They've admitted that is exactly what they would have done. If you think I have any spark of sympathy for Adam Powers, you're crazier than I think you are. I hope Mike gives him what he deserves."

Sam sat motionless for several seconds, his gaze on the banker's flushed face, his tight-lipped mouth, the hate-filled eyes. He rose as he said, "No, Jason, I'm not crazy enough to think you got any sympathy for my father."

As he walked out of the office, Small called after him, "You ought to thank Hale for saving your life. If he hadn't taken Adam off the stage, you'd be dead."

Sam strode across the lobby of the bank, not looking

at the teller, who stared at him with malicious triumph, and went on out into the morning sunshine. The fact that he had fully expected to get the answer he did in no way made it any easier to accept. Now he was left with no one to turn to, with no hope for a miracle.

Chapter 15

Julie Larkin had no intention of getting up until at least eight o'clock, but a drunken cowboy woke her just as the sun was beginning to show above the rim of the prairie to the east. He had tried one door after another along the hall, all the time singing "Home Sweet Home" in a booming voice.

Julie had locked her door, but it was a flimsy lock, and it would certainly not hold if he put his shoulder to the door and pushed. She got out of bed and propped her chair under the knob, then took her revolver from her suitcase and carried it back to bed. It was a small gun, but at close range it would inflict enough damage to stop a man unless he was bent on murder, and she had no reason to think he was.

When he reached her door, he tried the lock, still singing. He went on and must have found his room, or at least one that wasn't occupied, because a door banged open, then slammed shut, and that was the last she heard of him. He probably, she thought, had sprawled across a bed and had gone to sleep immediately. By that time Julie was completely awake and unable to get back to sleep.

She lay on her back staring at the ceiling as the light gradually deepened and the day was born. She thought of Tony Arbanz with amusement. He was a funny, intense little man who had responded to her compliments with complete trust and belief, as most men did. From the minute she got him into bed with her, she had so charmed him that he would have done anything she asked.

He was not the greatest lover she'd ever had in bed, but she had told him he was and he had believed her. He believed her, too, about being an editor who wanted to publish his book. She had gone to his print shop yesterday afternoon asking to see his manuscript. It was a perfectly logical request. She had a contract ready, she'd told him, and as soon as she heard from her New York office she would have the thousand dollars she had offered him as an advance.

At first Arbanz had made excuses, saying he had never let anyone see his manuscript except his daughter Betty, that it still needed some touching up here and there, but she had persisted, and after a hug and a couple of kisses, he had surrendered, taken the stack of papers from a desk drawer, and let her glance quickly through it.

It was all there, as Seth Alexander had suspected it would be. The book would play hell, she told herself, if it were printed. Not that Alexander and the other invaders would ever be brought to trial. The case had been dismissed.

The trouble was that the cowmen had tried and were still trying to present a law-abiding image to the public, pretending that the invasion had been an honest and necessary attempt to restore law on the Bensen County range, that the homesteaders had stolen the ranchers' stock until, like Adam Powers, they were broke. She did not read the manuscript carefully, but she read enough to see that Arbanz showed the invaders for what they were, vigilantes who had committed murder.

Despite her distaste for what she had read, she'd told him the book was great, that she wanted to publish it, and that it would sell thousands of copies. He was typical of men she had hypnotized. He had never asked to see her credentials or questioned her identity as an editor, but he had believed everything she'd told him. She suspected he was a violent man under the right circumstances, but that he wasn't as tough and worldly as most of the men she had met and conquered.

The only man she had ever tried to control and failed with was Seth Alexander. Thinking about him, she mentally conceded she had only partly failed. He was always willing to give her her way on minor matters, but in the end he controlled her on everything that counted.

That was why she was here, engaged in a scheme that was less than honorable. He had ordered her to come here and arrange for Tony Arbanz's murder. Not that she was opposed to anything that was dishonorable. It was just that this was the kind of business in which she could get herself killed. In the end she had agreed to everything he had asked of her, which included taking the long and tiring trip by stagecoach from Casper to Crow City.

She lay there motionless, breathing quietly, a stray beam of early morning sunlight falling on the wall beside her. She was very much aware that she could not go on living as she had been, jumping from one man to another, that the years were taking their toll, and that if she was ever going to provide for her future, she'd better be doing it. She'd collect all she could from Alexander when she got back to his ranch on the Sweetwater and leave him. He was, she knew, not a man she would ever succeed in luring to the altar.

Seth Alexander was a hard man, a big and brutal man, who'd had a succession of women living with him on his ranch on the Sweetwater. She was not the first and she would not be the last, although that was what she had hoped for. She had not been able to fully face up to the truth, but she did now.

She guessed she was a damned fool for going on living with Alexander and doing his dirty errands and never receiving any assurance that he would marry her, just some general promises that she was positive he never meant to keep.

This was the worst job he had given her. He had never before saddled her with murder. Well, now he had. Destroy Arbanz's manuscript if there was such a thing, although Alexander didn't really know he had written one. The main thing was to kill him so he could never put down in writing what he knew. He was the only man alive outside of the invaders themselves who knew the background and the planning of the invasion. He should, Alexander had said with heat, have died a long time ago.

She felt mildly sorry for Arbanz. He was a crusader, an idealist, but he was also a vindictive man who would destroy those who had fired him from his job as editor and physically abused him. Alexander sensed that. He had never given up the original plan of running the settlers out of Bensen County, or at least forcing them to give up their control of the county government.

Now Alexander knew a better way than the invasion, which had miserably failed. If it wasn't done soon, all of Wyoming would be overrun by the damned sodbusters. Martial law was the answer. An outbreak of violence could do the job.

Julie's purpose was twofold. First, she would see to it that the one man who could tell the public the full story of the invasion was dead. She could kill him herself or hire someone to do the job. If she decided to hire a man, Alexander recommended Mike Hale, who would, he said, steal the pennies off his grandmother's eyes after she had been laid to rest in her coffin. Hale hated him, Alexander said, but that wouldn't keep him from taking the job. Second, the killing could probably be blown into a panic that Alexander and his friends could use to persuade the governor to declare martial law in Bensen County.

She stretched and yawned, reminding herself that she had a long ride ahead of her today and she'd better get started. She rose and dressed, spending more time than was necessary on her black hair. Her hair was something Alexander had always admired. It was long, descending as far as her buttocks. It had always given him pleasure to sit and watch her take her hair down and brush it before they went to bed.

She smiled now as she thought about Alexander. She had never known another man who had been so enamored by her hair and she did not understand it. She had lived with him for two years, although he had been incarcerated in Cheyenne part of that time. They had been good years, she thought, as she pinned her hair up, but she told herself again that it was time to leave before she faded so much that he kicked her out. She would never get anything more from him than she was getting now. She had to keep reminding herself of that.

She went downstairs to breakfast, hoping she would not see Arbanz. He bored her now. She had gained his confidence and had found out all she needed to know. As soon as he was dead and the manuscript destroyed, she could catch the next stage to Casper. She would tarry briefly at the Sweetwater ranch and then go to Denver. Oh, she'd give him a chance to marry her, but she knew what his answer would be. She knew a banker in Denver who would marry her. She could have married him two years ago if Alexander had not come into her life.

The banker was old, but he was rich. Alexander was both rich and reasonably young; he had a strong animal magnetism about him that stirred her. She had never found it in another man. It was that as much as anything that let him persuade her to go with him to his Sweetwater ranch. She didn't regret her decision, but she realized at least that she could never bend him to her will, as she had other men she had lived with. Now she would go back to a man she knew she could handle.

As soon as she finished breakfast, she returned to her room, put on her brown riding skirt, tan blouse, and leather jacket. She slipped her revolver into her jacket pocket. Alexander had warned her about Hale. He was an animal, and she should never give him the slightest advantage. "Kill him if you have to, but don't let him get a hand on you," Alexander had said. She knew exactly what he'd meant. She had, to her regret, met men like Mike Hale.

She went down the stairs and across the lobby into the bright morning sunshine. She had made arrangements the previous afternoon at the Red Front livery stable to rent a saddle horse and hire the owner, Art Palmer, to guide her to Mike Hale's ranch.

The horses were saddled and waiting when she reached the stable. Palmer looked at her sourly as he said, "You're half an hour late, ma'am."

She was irritated, and a sharp answer was on the tip of her tongue until she remembered that she'd had trouble the day before finding someone who would take her to Hale's place. Palmer had agreed only after much persuasion and after she had raised her offer from fifteen to twenty-five dollars for the trip.

She hesitated until she could say in a civil tone, "I'm sorry. I overslept."

Palmer shrugged and let it go at that. He gave her a hand up, then mounted, and turned east, Julie following. They rode in silence, taking the county road for several miles, then swinging southeast across the trackless prairie. They dropped down into Dry Creek canyon, and when they reached the cottonwood grove, Julie was tempted to dismount and rest in the shade. She was used to riding, but not for this long.

"How much farther is it?" she asked.

"Ain't far," he answered.

She nodded and they rode on, Julie deciding she'd rest on the way back to town. She found herself worrying about the meeting with Hale, mentally going over what she would say to him. None of the words that came to her seemed quite right.

She glanced at Palmer, riding beside her. He was an old man, tight-lipped, with a tanned, lined face. He probably had been a homesteader, she thought, and had grown tired of his gamble with the United States government and had decided to try a sure thing. He would be of no help if she had trouble with Hale, and she knew that was a distinct possibility. Hale had an explosive temper, Alexander had said, and he had warned her that Hale might explode when she mentioned Seth Alexander's name.

Palmer pointed ahead to a shack and slab barn and corral. "That's it," he said. "About as near nothing as you'll find, even for a homesteader." He shot her a questioning glance, then added, "Now it ain't none of my business, but what do you want with an ornery son like Mike Hale?"

She smiled sweetly and said, "You're right, Mr. Palmer. It ain't none of your business."

He shrugged, apparently not offended. He said, "You'll be lucky to find him. Usually he's out cavorting around somewhere, stealing somebody's cows if he can find 'em, or horses if they're handy."

"Why didn't you tell me before we started?" she demanded.

He shrugged again. "You didn't ask. Besides, I needed the twenty-five dollars your offered."

She was thoroughly angry then. She snapped. "You're impossible, Mr. Palmer. Utterly impossible."

His wrinkled face broke into a grin. "I know that, ma'am. My wife tells me every day that I'm just what you say."

In spite of herself Julie smiled. "You're honest anyway." A few minutes later, when they were within fifty yards of the shack, she said, "You stay here. My talk with Hale is private, but wait for me. I'd never find my way back to town and I don't want to stay here any longer than necessary."

He hesitated. "I don't cotton to that notion, ma'am. Like I said, Hale is an ornery son. Don't trust him."

"I won't," she said. "I'll only be a few minutes if I'm lucky enough to find him."

He reined up and watched her as she rode toward Hale's shack, a worried frown creasing his forehead.

Chapter 16

Sam could think of a dozen things that needed to be done around the AP, but he was too restless to stay with anything. He started to clean out the barn, then threw the pitchfork down and walked out, leaving the wheelbarrow filled with manure in the runway. He went around the house to the woodpile and started to chop wood for the kitchen range, but ended up sinking the ax back into the chopping block with the job half done.

He walked aimlessly around the barn and corrals, then saw Bronc Collins coming in from the horse pasture, a hammer and bucket of staples in his hands. When Bronc reached him, Sam said, "When is Hale going to make his move?"

Bronc shrugged. "Dunno, but it won't be till after sundown. You can count on that."

Sam heard his mother ring the dinner bell and turned toward the house. Bronc left the hammer and staples in the barn and caught up with him. He said, "Sam, maybe I'm looking on the dark side of this business, but I know Mike Hale well enough to guess that Adam's dead."

Sam nodded. "I had the same hunch, but until we know, we got to be ready to do something."

"Do what?" Bronc asked caustically. "You didn't do no good with Jason Small. You can't raise five cents. Money's what Hale's interested in and that's all he's interested in."

"I know, I know," Sam said irritably. "We got to try to trick him into telling us where Pa is, maybe give him a sack of cut-up newspaper."

They went into the kitchen and washed up at the

sink. Sam knew from Bronc's silence that he didn't think much of Sam's idea. Sam didn't, either, but any idea was better than nothing. After his search yesterday, nothing was exactly what he had.

They ate in silence, Ida Powers watching Sam apprehensively. When he pushed back his plate and shook his head at her offer of another cup of coffee, she said, "You didn't eat enough to keep a bird alive. You're going to make yourself sick."

"It's not me making me sick," he said. "It's Hale. Pa, too, I reckon. If he was in my place, he'd do something. I dunno what, but he'd do something."

"He never had to face a situation like this," Ida said. "He used to say he wouldn't play if he didn't have an ace in the hole."

"That's right," Bronc added. "He was big enough and tough enough to make his own rules most of the time. When it got so he couldn't, he fretted himself into going crazy and joining up with the invaders."

Sam hadn't thought of it that way, but it was true that nearly all cattlemen played by their rules and refused to recognize any others. As far back as he could remember, until recently, Adam Powers had arrogantly considered himself above the problems and troubles of the average man.

Seth Alexander and most of the other cattlemen in the state still considered themselves to be in the same position. So far Adam was the only one who had been ruined by rustlers, but the others had seen what had happened to him and had been panicked into taking the law into their own hands.

The cattlemen had lost the legal machinery of Bensen County, but to all intents and purposes they still controlled the state government. They were still arrogant, in spite of the way the invasion had turned out; they still felt they were above the troubles and problems that afflicted the average citizen.

"I'll take that cup of coffee, Ma," Sam said. "Betty told me that her pa has written a book telling all he knew about the invasion. If Seth Alexander and his friends know that, even guess it, they'll do anything to keep his book from being published." He picked up the cup of coffee that his mother had poured then drank and set the cup down. "Of course that's got nothing to do with what's happening to Pa."

Ida frowned as she considered what Sam had said. She sat down and laid her hands on the table. She asked, "Where is the book now—I mean, whatever Arbanz has written?"

"I dunno," Sam said. "He took it home last night and stayed up most of the night working on it. Maybe he left it home."

"I'm worried about Betty," Ida said. "Sometimes I get a feeling about things like that, but I thought it was just because I was worried about Adam. I don't really care about Tony Arbanz, but I do care about Betty. You go tell her to come over here and spend the night."

"I've tried to talk her into coming here before," Sam said, "but I'll try again."

He rose and left the house, more upset by what his mother had said than he wanted to admit. He'd known of too many occasions in the past when his mother's forebodings had turned out to be right. He saddled up and rode to Betty's house, thinking that while there was no connection between what had happened to Adam and the arrival of the Larkin woman in Crow City, the entire pattern of life in Bensen County crackled so much with crosscurrents of human emotion that the climate was as ripe for murder as it had been before the invasion.

The situation would remain that way until the cattlemen stopped their plotting and known rustlers like Mike Hale were driven out of the county. He had no way of knowing when the former would happen, but the latter had just about been accomplished. Hale and his friends, the Martins, were, as far as Sam knew, the only ones left in the county.

He found Betty as restless as he had been all day. She fled into the safety of his arms and clutched him with a fierceness he had seldom felt in her. "Sam, Sam," she whispered. "I know how you're feeling. I can't stand waiting for something terrible to happen. All I know is that it's going to. I guess with Adam it's already happened."

She began to cry. He held her in his arms for a long time, thinking that Tony Arbanz had decreed his fate when he had come to Crow City to play the role of a firebrand. Adam had done the same for himself when he had chosen to join the invaders.

Betty drew back from Sam and wiped her eyes. "I'm sorry," she said, "but I guess I was bottled up. I feel better." She gripped Sam's arms. "Listen. I don't suppose it'll do any good, but I want to go see the Larkin woman. Will you go with me?"

"No, it won't do any good," he said. "She won't admit she's here to fleece your pa."

"We can ask her for her credentials," Betty said. "If she's honest, she'll have contracts and correspondence to show she's an editor."

Sam shrugged. "All right, we'll try it. Sure can't hurt anything. I'll saddle up for you."

They rode to Crow City in silence, each caught up in thoughts that were not pleasant. At least, Sam told himself, it gave Betty something to do and that was good. Good for him, he thought. Certainly better than wandering around the AP waiting out the slow hours.

Now that he looked back on yesterday's search, he regretted that he hadn't worked Hale over and forced him to tell what he had done with Adam. The way he felt now, he'd torture the man or do anything that would get the information he wanted. If he didn't hear today, that was exactly what he would do tomorrow.

Maybe it was just as well he hadn't attempted anything of the sort yesterday. He wasn't sure whether Ed Garber would have stood for it. Sam would never have considered that sort of pressure if anyone beside his father had been involved.

They reined up in front of the hotel, dismounted, then tied and went into the lobby. John Doyle, who was behind the desk, nodded a greeting and asked, "What brings you to town?"

"We want to talk to Julie Larkin," Betty said. "Which room is she in?"

"Well now," Doyle said, "I'm sorry about that, but she's out. She left tolerably early this morning. She didn't say nothing to me, but a little later I seen her riding out of town with Art Palmer."

"Which direction?" Sam asked.

"Going east," Doyle answered.

"No idea when she'll be back?" Betty asked.

"Not any," Doyle said. "Like I told you, she never said a word to me. Just walked out."

"Did she ever say anything to you about what her work was," Betty asked, "and why she was here?"

Doyle frowned. "Yes and no. She told me right off that she was Bud Larkin's sister and had come to find out more about why and how he was killed. But as far as what she did, no, she never opened her mouth."

Betty hesitated. She glanced at Sam, as if wanting his approval for her questions, but he was looking at Doyle. She swallowed and went on, "Mr. Doyle, please don't think I'm being pushy, but I've got a reason for asking questions about her. Did she ask anything about the town or the people?"

"Oh, yes," Doyle answered. "Yesterday just before breakfast she asked if I knew your pa and I said yes, that he'd just gone into the dining room. She went in and sat down at his table, and afterwards they went upstairs to her room. They came in together in the afternoon and went up to her room again for about an hour. I don't know what their business was."

"Oh," Betty said, as if her breath had been jolted out of her. She turned to the door, then called back, "Thank you."

Sam remained behind to ask, "One more thing, John. There's a lot going on that we don't know about, but it worries us and we're doing some guessing. Did she ever show any interest in Mike Hale?"

"Yeah, she asked me yesterday morning where he

113

lived," Doyle answered, "and then last night about bed-
time she came downstairs and asked if Art Palmer was
dependable. I told her he was. I thought about that
this morning when they rode off together. Maybe it's
got nothing to do with Hale, but they was headed that
way."

"Thanks, John," Sam said, and joined Betty on
the boardwalk. "You want to talk to Ed Garber before
we leave town?"

She shook her head, her lips tightly pressed together.
"The woman hasn't committed any crime yet that we
know of." She clutched his arm. "Sam, why would
they go up to her room?"

Sam could think of one very good reason, but he
didn't want to tell Betty. He shook his head. "Dunno.
Ready to go home?"

"I'm ready," she said. "That woman is bad medicine.
I wish I hadn't asked Doyle all those questions."

Sam didn't say anything as he gave her a hand up,
but he knew she had thought of the same reason he
had for her father going to Julie's room.

Chapter 17

As Julie Larkin approached Mike Hale's place, she
saw two men hunkered in the scant noon shade. They
were whittling, their hat brims pulled down over their
eyes. They pretended they didn't see her coming, but
she sensed they were watching every move she made.
She didn't rein up until she was about twenty feet from
them.

They looked up suddenly, as if surprised that she
was there. "What do you know," the squat man said.

"A female woman. Now ain't she a long ways from home?"

They rose, tossing the sticks they were whittling to one side. "By God, Mike," the lanky one said. "She is a woman. I reckon she's female, but mebbe we ought to find out."

For a moment panic rushed through Julie as her right hand dropped into the pocket of her coat and gripped the butt of her gun. She had told herself she could handle any man, but suddenly she realized she could not handle two, and Art Palmer would be of no help whatever.

She pinned her gaze on Hale's face and drew in a long breath. "I assume you're Mike Hale."

He grinned as he cuffed his hat back on his forehead. "I'm Hale, sweetheart," he said. "If you're here to see me, get down off your horse and come in. It sure is a relief to look at your purty face after staring at this bastard's ugly mug all morning."

"No, I'll stay here," she said. "My business won't take long. Send your man away. What I have to say to you is private."

The panic returned as she became aware that these were probably two of the three men who had kidnapped Adam Powers. Their sizes and shapes corresponded exactly with the kidnappers. Their faces had been masked, but now she was certain that Hale's voice was the same as the man's who had given directions when Powers had been taken off the stage.

She had no idea whether or not they recognized her, but if they did, they would probably kill her rather than let her go back to Crow City to identify them. She had come this far, so she'd do her errand, she told herself, as her grip tightened on the butt of the gun, but she must not give the slightest indication that she had recognized them.

Hale's grin widened as he licked his lips. She was reminded of a giant bulldog that runs his red tongue over his protruding jaws before he tackles a meat-covered bone. He jerked his thumb at the lanky man.

115

"Vamoose, Marty," Hale said. "Our purty visitor cottons to me, not you."

"Oh hell," the lanky man said in disgust. "It ain't right. Everything comes your way."

As he moved around the corner of the shed, Julie said, "I'm Julie Larkin, Bud's sister."

Hale's mouth popped open and his eyes widened in astonishment; then he slapped his leg and guffawed. "Now I hate to tell a purty thing like you that you're a liar, but that's sure as hell what you are. I knew old Bud purty well, and I know he didn't have no sister. He was the only kid in his family."

The weakness of panic surged through her again, so violently that she thought she was going to be sick. Alexander had told her to claim that she was Bud's sister, but he had not told her that Bud didn't have a sister. Probably he hadn't known and had not throught that Hale would know.

"It doesn't make any difference," Julie said, struggling to hold the same tone of voice. "I tell the people in town that I'm Bud's sister and nobody knows the difference. As long as I'm in this country, I'll continue claiming that identity. I'm here to offer you a job that will pay you $1,000. Are you interested?"

The grin left his mouth and his eyes narrowed. He said, "Hell, ma'am, only the worst kind of a fool would say no to any offer like that, but likewise a man would be the worst kind of a fool if he said yes to a job before he knew what it was."

"Good," she said. "I'm Seth Alexander's housekeeper and I do different jobs . . ."

"Housekeeper?" He laughed. "Housekeeper, you say? I guess you do different jobs for him, all right. By God, that's the funniest thing I ever heard. You couldn't boil water. I've heard of you. You're Alexander's whore."

She stiffened, her face turning red. She hated the word and she never allowed herself to think she was one. She was too smart and too pretty to be a whore. She liked to think of herself as Alexander's companion.

Or mistress. She preferred that. She had read the word in a novel and she loved the sound and implication of it.

"I'm not here to be insulted, Hale," she said haughtily, her chin thrust out at a belligerent angle. "If you don't want to keep a civil tongue in your head, I'll go back to town."

He grinned. "I apologize, ma'am. I didn't have no idea you were that touchy. Now about that high-paying job?"

"Alexander wants Tony Arbanz killed," she said, "and the manuscript of his book turned over to me. I have the first $500 with me, and I'll give it to you when you agree to do the job. When you're finished, report to me and you'll get the other $500."

For a moment Hale said nothing, his eyes probing the girl, as if he were puzzled about something. He said, "This is the damnedest thing I ever heard of. Alexander ran me and my brother Lon off his range and he helped murder Lon. He would have strung me up if he could have caught me long enough to put a rope on my neck, but now he wants to hire me to do a job of killing."

"He said he hated you and you hated him," Julie said, "but he also said that didn't change the color of his money."

"I'll agree to that," Hale said, nodding. "Now why does he want Tony Arbanz beefed? I've got nothing against Tony. Fact is, I kind of like the little bastard."

"He seldom tells me the reasons when he wants something done," Julie said. "Besides, his reasons are no business of yours."

Hale shrugged his sholders. "All right, I'll take your money. When do you want it done?"

"Today," she answered. "Or tonight. I want to catch tomorrow's stage. I'm staying at the hotel. If I'm not in the lobby or the dining room, tell Doyle to get me. Arbanz will probably be in his shop tonight. If not, he'll be home. I understand he lives just a couple of miles out of town."

"It's a deal," Hale said.

"The manuscript is in the top drawer of his office desk," she said. "Don't forget to bring it to me. You won't get paid if you don't have it."

"I'll get it," he said, and started walking toward her. "If you're good enough for Alexander, you're good enough for me. We might as well get friendly, so get down off . . ."

Her gun was in her hand before he had taken two steps. "I'd as soon kill you as any rattlesnake I ever saw," she said. "I don't think there's much difference."

He stopped, a grudging expression of admiration coming into his face. "So, our spitfire has a bite with her bark," he said. "Well, it's your loss."

"Here's twenty-five double eagles," she said as she tossed a buckskin bag to him.

She wheeled her horse and rode away, not putting her gun back into her pocket until she was fifty yards from Hale. She told herself bitterly that Seth Alexander either was a fool or he didn't give a damn about her. He should have sent a man for a job like this. She didn't draw a full breath until she rode up beside Art Palmer.

"I see you're still in one piece," Palmer said, staring at her pale face. He turned his horse to ride beside her, adding, "I wasn't real sure you would be."

She didn't say anything until her heart had stopped pounding. When she did, her voice trembled in spite of herself. She said, "I wasn't sure, either. What kind of a reputation does Hale have around town?"

"He pretends to be a homesteader," Palmer answered, "but everybody knows he's a horse thief and cattle rustler. Trouble was we was all glad to have a hard case like him on our side when the invaders showed up, so I guess folks put up with him because of that. He's a bad man, miss, the worst in the county."

"Why didn't you tell me that?" she demanded angrily, as if he was the cause of the danger that now seemed more real than ever, as she thought of the way Mike Hale had looked at her.

"I wanted to," Palmer said, "but you strike me as a headstrong young woman. I didn't figger you'd listen to anything I had to say."

"No, I guess I wouldn't have." She sighed, suddenly realizing that she was tired and hungry and thirsty. Scared, too. "When we get back to those trees, I want to stop and rest. Is there any water close by?"

He nodded. "There's a spring in the lower part of the canyon. The water's good if there is any. Trouble is, it dries up later in the summer, but I reckon it'll still be flowing this early."

She wiped her face with a handkerchief, thinking of words she would use on Seth Alexander the next time she saw him. They would not be polite words. He had paid her a niggardly amount to go to Crow City, and she'd get twice that much out of him or he'd be sorry he had ever picked her for a job as dangerous as this.

When they reached the canyon, Palmer reined up. "The spring is just yonder," he said. "I don't reckon we'd better stay here very long, so get down and have your drink and we'll mosey on."

"I'm tired," she snapped. "I want to rest here in the shade."

"Then you'll be resting alone," he said uneasily as he glanced back the way they come. "Hale may get to thinking what you looked like and decide he'd made a mistake letting you go. I seen a girl in Crow City that he'd used. It wasn't a purty sight, ma'am."

She stood beside her horse for a moment, staring at Art Palmer's worried face. She knew he was right. Tired or not, she'd go on. She said, "All right, I'll get my drink and we'll keep riding."

Leaving the reins dragging, she knelt beside the spring, a pool of clear, cool water. Putting her cupped hands into the spring, she lifted them to her mouth. The next instant a rifle cracked and a bullet slapped into the ground not more than two feet from her, a small geyser of dirt and leaves exploding beside her. Her horse would have bolted if Palmer hadn't grabbed the reins.

"Climb on," Palmer yelled. "We've got to get out of here."

She remained frozen for a few seconds, her body refusing to obey the mental command to get up and mount her horse. Then she thought, "He'll ride off without me if I stay here." That broke the trance. She scrambled to her feet, her heart pounding as hard as it had when she had left Mike Hale. The affair was turning out even worse than she had thought, but there didn't seem to be any logic in Hale shooting at her. She mounted and took the reins.

"Keep close to the north wall," Palmer barked, and dug steel into his horse.

She slapped her animal with the end of the reins and the horse started to run. She had very little control over him, but he stayed directly behind Palmer's horse, and Palmer was staying off the trail and as close to the base of the north wall as he could.

They didn't slow up until they reached the west end of the canyon; then Palmer looked back as he pulled his horse down to a walk. He raised a hand and shouted, "We can take it easy now. That shot wasn't intended to kill us. Just to get us out of there in a hurry."

Julie didn't speak until they'd ridden a mile across the prairie. She wasn't sure she believed what Palmer had said about the shot being a warning. She had never been shot at before, and for that mile she wasn't sure whether her heart would slow down to normal or not.

When she could speak, she asked, "Why? We weren't hurting anything."

"I dunno why," Palmer answered, "but somebody didn't want us hanging around the bottom of the canyon. If we'd just ridden through, he probably wouldn't have fired the shot. I reckon there's something there somebody didn't want us to see, but I ain't interested in finding out what. We'll let the sheriff look into that."

Julie told herself she didn't care who it was or why,

or whether it had anything to do with her seeing Mike Hale. She was just glad to get out of the canyon alive. One thing was sure. She wasn't going to demand twice as much as Seth Alexander had given her. He was going to pay her three times as much.

Chapter 18

Mike Hale stood motionless as he watched Julie Larkin ride away, a crazy wildness of temper building up in him. He didn't move until after she had joined Art Palmer. Marty Martin, who had come around the corner of the shed, stopped and looked at him, an expression of mild amusement on his thin face.

"I thought you was going to pull her off her horse and take her into the house," Martin said. "She looked like she'd be mighty interesting in bed."

"She's spent plenty of time there," Hale snapped. "By God, she had the gall to claim she was insulted when I called her a whore. Hell, that's all she has been for at least the two years she's been living with Alexander. Called herself a housekeeper."

"There's some that's proud to be called whores and some that ain't," Martin said. "All depends what grade they're on. That one looked like an A Number One."

"She'd have to be to satisfy Alexander," Hale said. "He can afford the best." Then he shrugged and added, "Oh well, I guess we don't want any of Alexander's leftovers."

"You're sore because you didn't get a piece," Martin said. "I still don't know why you just didn't pick her out of her saddle and carry her . . ."

"Because she had a gun on me," Hale exploded. "I

could tell by looking at her that she'd have put a window in my skull if I'd touched her. But I'll get her before I leave this country. By God, I'll get her good. She'll be sorry she got so damned uppity with me."

"What are you talking about, leaving this country?" Martin demanded. "I thought we had it all to ourselves here. Don't look to me like it's any time to leave."

"That's because you ain't as smart as I am," Hale said. "It's time, all right. All of a sudden the sheriff gets an attack of guts and comes out here looking for trouble. As far as having it all to ourselves, that's the trouble. If we stole a jag of cattle, they'd all know who done it."

"I don't figger Garber's gonna have another attack of guts very soon," Martin said. "Young Powers was egging him on. He'll never do it again."

Hale shook his head. "You're dead wrong, Marty. Once a bastard like Garber does something big, he gets the notion that the real Ed Garber's a tough hand. I figgered he'd go on thinking I was just like the other homesteaders and he'd bend the law in my favor like he's been doing, but no, he's got to throw in with Powers."

Hale picked up the buckskin bag that Julie had tossed to him, then turned and walked to the house, Martin falling into step with him.

"Just where'd you figure to go that'd be any better'n Wyoming?" Martin demanded.

"I dunno," Hale answered. "All I know is I'm tired of this country. I'll earn the rest of Alexander's dinero, then we'll collect from Powers, and we'll be on our way."

"To where?" Martin demanded doggedly. "I'm wanted in about ten states. Wyoming happens to be where I ain't."

"Grow a beard and nobody'll know you," Hale said. "I figgered we'd head for Oregon or Washington. Lots of big, empty country in both states. We'll have enough dinero to buy us a small spread. Maybe it's time we started working for a living."

Martin snorted. "You was born to hang, Mike. You couldn't keep your hands off your neighbors' cows no matter what state you're in."

Hale paced back and forth in front of the house, his eyes on the ground. Presently he stooped and picked up a fist-sized rock and went inside, saying absentmindedly, "We'll see. We'll see."

Martin stood in the doorway watching Hale take a piece of paper out of his pocket, wrap it around the rock, and then tie it securely with a length of string.

"Have you gone loco?" Martin demanded. "What kind of a game are you playing now?"

"This is a message from old man Powers to the family," Hale said. "Likewise my orders when and where to leave the money. We're pulling out first thing tomorrow morning after Powers leaves the dinero in Dry Creek Canyon."

He pushed past Martin into the afternoon sunlight, glanced at the sun, and made an estimate of the hours of daylight that were left. He said, "I'm sending your boy with this note to the Powers place. I'm heading for town. I may not be back until after I pick up Powers' money. You heard the woman's offer?"

"I heard," Martin said sullenly, "and I don't like it one damn bit. We got nothing against Arbanz, and I sure don't cotton to the notion of doing Alexander's dirty work for him."

"For $1,000 I ain't gonna be choosy about whose dirty work I do," Hale said. "If I can find that book Arbanz is supposed to be writing, we can milk Alexander for a fortune. Anyhow, you get the grub packed. Dig up the dinero we've got cached under the floor. We're leaving here with a purty good stake. It'll give us a start in Oregon."

Hale stopped, his eyes narrowing. "Marty, we've been partners for quite a spell, but I never seen a man who wouldn't take advantage of a pal where money was involved. I'll tell you one thing you've got to believe. If you double-cross me and head out of here with everything we've saved for the last two or three years, you'll never see your kid alive again."

Martin's face turned red. "By God, Mike, I oughtta knock you pizzle end up. I never double-crossed a partner in my life and I ain't starting now. It makes me damned sore that you'd even . . ."

"All right, all right," Hale said. "I just wanted to be sure you savvied."

He wheeled away, strode to the corral, and caught and saddled his horse. He mounted and rode toward Dry Creek Canyon, not looking back at Martin, who stood motionless in front of the house, staring truculently at him. Hale had learned the truth of the old adage about there being no honor among thieves. He never trusted anyone, and he didn't trust Martin now, but he was sure that the threat against Martin's son would be enough to keep the man honest.

Presently he left the Dry Creek Canyon road and swung north, then west to follow the trail along the rim. A few minutes later the Martin boy saw him coming and rose from where he had been hunkered among the rocks.

"Where you headed, Mike?" the boy asked. "I didn't figger on seeing you today."

Hale reined up and handed the boy the rock with the paper wrapped around it. He said, "Something came up so I've got to go to town. I want you to ride to the Powers place. Get close enough to the house so you can throw this rock through one of their front windows, then bust the breeze getting out of there. They may take a shot at you, but if you get a move on, you'll be out of range before any of 'em think of getting a gun."

The boy hefted the rock and turned it over in his hand. He said hesitantly, "I'll do it, Mike, but I don't like the idea. I don't think I oughtta leave here."

"Why not?"

"It's hard to tell who'll come riding by," the boy answered. "Art Palmer and a woman I didn't know rode through here a little while ago. I seen 'em first mebee an hour before riding toward our place. I had my sights on 'em, but they kept riding, so I didn't take a crack at 'em, but when they came back, they stopped at the spring and the woman got off her horse to get a drink. I figgered if they stayed a while, they might get to nosing around and we'd be in trouble, so I dropped a slug in close to where the woman was squatting beside the spring."

The boy snickered. "You should of seen 'em. Palmer yelled to get out of there, but the woman was too scared to move for a spell. I'll bet she wet her pants. Then she came to life, got into saddle, and they went out of there like a bat out of hell." He paused, then added regretfully, "Hell, Mike, I could of beefed both of 'em, but I remembered what you said."

"Good boy," Hale said. "You done just right. Now you light a shuck out of here. We'll take a chance on anybody else riding by."

"What is this?" the boy asked, hefting the rock again.

"A note I got old man Powers to write telling 'em he's alive," Hale said. "I put down how much we want and where to leave it."

"How much?" the boy asked.

Hale hesitated, thinking it was none of the kid's business how much he was asking, but the boy was in the game along with his father. No sense kicking up any dust yet. That would come later when they were out of the country. He had no intention of sharing with them, but they didn't know that, and there was no sense in making them suspicious.

"$5,000," Hale said. "I'm telling 'em to bring it here at sunup tomorrow. Sam's to come alone. I expect you to be here and finish him as soon as he drops the money. I'll rub the old man out and we'll be on our way. I told your pa we'd head for Oregon."

"I'd like that," the boy said, nodding. "I'm getting damned tired of this country. I've been sitting here in the sun too long." He looked at the rock again and shook his head. "Mike, it ain't gonna work. By the time they get this, it'll be too late to go to the bank and you know they ain't got no $5,000 laying around their house."

"They'll get it if they have to rob the bank," Hale said. "I know Sam Powers well enough to know that. Chances are they'll trot Ames down to the bank no matter what time it is." He started to ride on, then pulled his horse to a stop. "I hope you can throw purty good."

The boy grinned. "I can throw purty good, all right. That don't bother me. I just hope I can outride the bullets they send after me."

"Get out of there in a hurry and you'll be all right," Hale said. "Be sure you come back here. I'll stop by and see you on my way home, but it'll be after dark, so I'll see you in the canyon."

He nodded at the boy and rode on, well pleased with himself. It was working out better than he had hoped. He'd been ready for a year to move on to greener pastures, but he had waited, hoping something would turn up that would add to his stake.

He'd made enough out of his rustling and horse stealing to buy a big outfit in Oregon, but a couple of binges in Sheridan and one in Billings had taken most of it. Women and poker had been his undoing, but now it was going to be all right.

Suddenly he laughed aloud. Tough, loud-talking Seth Alexander was helping pay his way out of the country, but old Seth wasn't done paying. Not, Hale told himself, if he could find Arbanz's book that Julie Larkin was talking about. No, Alexander wasn't done paying. Not by a long shot.

Chapter 19

Neither Sam nor Betty felt like talking as they rode back to the Arbanz place from Crow City. Sam knew that Betty's thoughts were on her father and Julie Larkin, but his mind was on a more pressing problem, one that had to be solved soon.

He could not allow her to stay alone in her house, but he had tried before to get her to go home with him and she had refused. She was, he had learned on a number of occasions, a very stubborn woman on matters that were important to her. The trouble was he didn't know how important this was. Well, he'd soon find out.

When they reached her house, they reined up and Sam stepped down. He gave her a hand, then said, "I'll take care of the horses later," and followed her into the house. He sensed she was curious about what he was going to do, but he didn't say anything until he took his hat off and sailed it across the room to the leather couch and dropped into a chair.

She stood in the center of the room, her hands on her hips, a quizzical smile on her lips. "Just what are your plans, Mr. Sam Powers? You planning to stay for supper?"

"Thought I would," he said. "You see, I want you to come home with me, but you've said no. I ain't leaving you here alone. What happens to you is more important to me than what happens to Pa or whether Tony goes back to see Julie Larkin."

She sat down, her troubled gaze on his face. "I'll be all right," she said. "I'm sorry I worry you so much."

"There's nobody in the world I'd rather worry about," he said. "I used to dream about meeting the right girl, but I guess I never really thought I'd ever do it. I figured I'd have to settle for some flibber gibbet of a town girl or some fat homesteader's daughter. Then you came along and I didn't have no trouble knowing if you were the right girl. I think I knew it the first time I saw you."

She laughed, then her face turned grave. "It makes me happy to hear you say those nice things, but how do you know I'm in any danger staying here?"

"Just a hunch," he said. "Hale is the kind of man who would go to hell and back to get even. The last thing he said to me was that he'd get me and for me not to forget it. If he can't get at me, you'll be the next best thing."

She shook her head. "I won't be alone. Daddy always comes home."

"You might just as well face it," Sam said. "He might spend the night with the Larkin woman. I guess it's what Ma said that worries me. She's got a bad feeling about you staying here. I've seen too many of her bad feelings come true not to pay attention to them. Mebbe it sounds crazy, but she does have second sight, whatever that means."

Betty rose and walked to a window. "I don't believe in that kind of thing."

"You haven't lived with Ma all your life like I have," he said. "Now I can't pick you up and carry you to my place, so I'm going to do the only other thing I can. I'm staying here all night. I guess you might as well start supper."

He wasn't sure how she would take this. He didn't want to make her angry, but he didn't know what else to do or say. She didn't move for a full minute, and then she turned slowly, a small smile on her lips, and he knew there would be no more trouble.

"You are a very stubborn man, Sam," she said. "I guess I'll just have to adjust to that fact if we're going to live together for the next fifty years."

"I thank you," he said, bowing to her. "I'm happy that you're not stubborn."

She giggled. "Of course I'm not stubborn," she said, and disappeared into her bedroom.

They left a few minutes later, Sam carrying Betty's small bag in front of him. She looked at him and then turned her head. Something was troubling her, but not knowing what it was, he waited until she brought it up.

They had almost reached the AP when she said, "Sam, I don't want to be any bother to your mother."

"You won't be," he said. "She's been after me to bring you here long enough. You can help her with the meals and there's an extra bed upstairs. The room's next to mine."

"Well," she said sharply, "don't expect that to do you any good."

He groaned. "I was afraid it wouldn't."

She glanced at him sharply, as if she were not sure how he meant it, then she said, "Sam, sometimes you make me so mad I can taste it. You're going to have to tell me when you're joshing."

"You'll be able to read me like a book after we've been married twenty years," he said.

"I doubt it," she snapped.

When they reached the AP, he said, "We'll leave the horses out here until after we go in, then I'll come out and take care of 'em."

They walked up the path to the front porch, Sam opening the screen door and holding it for Betty to go ahead. He called, "Ma, Betty's here."

They waited until Ida Powers came out of the kitchen, Bronc Collins behind her. She was holding a scrap of wrinkled paper in one hand. She had been crying, but she dabbed at her eyes with a wadded-up handkerchief and said, "I'm glad you're here, Betty. I've been worried sick about you being alone so much."

She handed Sam the paper. "We got this a while ago." She pointed to a broken window. "Through there. It was wrapped around a rock."

Sam hadn't noticed that a window had been broken, but now he saw the splintered pane and fragments of glass on the rag rug. He swore softly. "That's one way to deliver a letter," he said. "Who did it?"

"Dunno," Bronc said. "I was chopping wood for your ma when I heard her scream. I ran around the house in time to see this jasper busting the breeze out of here. I didn't know what he'd done, but I knew it wasn't anything good or he wouldn't be riding like that, so I threw a shot at him, but hell, he was too far away by that time. I ran into the house and got your pa's Winchester, but then he wasn't much more'n a dot out there on the grass."

Sam flattened out the wrinkled paper and read the scrawled words: "Pay it. Adam Powers." Below it was a second message in a different handwriting: "Bring $5,000 tomorrow at sunup to the west end of Dry Creek Canyon. Drop it at the base of the third cottonwood then vamoose. You'll never see the old man alive if you hang around or if you ain't there with the dinero."

"The first part is Pa's handwriting, all right," Sam said. "At least he was alive when he wrote it."

Bronc nodded. "Whether he's alive now is something else."

Sam turned to his mother. "Did you know the fellow who threw the rock?"

She shook her head. "I was in the kitchen making a cake. I hoped Betty would come back with you and I wanted something nice for her to eat. I heard the glass break and ran into the living room. The glass was all over the floor. I looked out and I saw this man . . . I think he was just a boy . . . riding away. At least he was awful skinny for a grown man, but he was tall enough." She dabbed at her eyes again and swallowed. "I don't remember screaming, but Bronc says he heard me."

Betty moved to Ida and put an arm around her. "Let's go finish the cake, Mrs. Powers. It was awfully nice of you to think of baking it for me."

They walked into the kitchen, Sam watching them until they disappeared and thinking how well Betty understood the situation. It was the best thing in the world for his mother to keep busy. She might not love Adam Powers, but the thought of him being murdered in cold blood was more than she could bear.

"Well?" Bronc asked. "What are we going to do?"

"All we can do is to go ahead with what we talked about," Sam said. "We figgered it would go something like this. We just didn't know where to take our sack of cut-up paper."

"For all the good it'll do," Bronc grumbled. "Adam's dead, Sam. We'll be running the risk of getting beefed, and for nothing."

"I figger you're right," Sam admitted, "but at least we may get a crack at Hale. It must have been the Martin kid who threw the rock."

Bronc scratched the back of his neck, acting as if he wanted to say something and was afraid to say it. Sam turned to the door, saying, "I'd better put the horses away."

"I'll do it," Bronc said, then he blurted, "Sam, when I read that note telling us to leave the money in Dry Creek Canyon, I thought of something I should have thought of before. You'n Garber rode through Dry Creek Canyon on your way to Hale's, didn't you?"

"Yeah, but what's that got to do with anything?" Sam asked. "It's the way the road goes to Hale's from town, if you want to call it a road. I dunno why we're supposed to leave the money there unless Hale thinks he can hide in the trees and knock me off after I drop the sack."

"I'm guessing he's been holding Adam there," Bronc said. "That's what I just thought of and you're gonna be sore at me for not thinking of it sooner. You didn't notice no cabins or dugouts or soddies or anything when you rode through there?"

"Hell no," Sam said. "What are you getting at? There's some brush growing along the north canyon wall and the cottonwoods. Then there's that spring at the lower end of the canyon and some willows growing around it. I never heard of anybody living there, so we didn't even think of looking for a dugout. We'd have seen a cabin or a soddy if one had been there."

"There's a dugout," Bronc said. "That's what I should have thought about, but it was a long time ago. You was too young to remember, or it might have been before you was born. Anyhow, an old goat named Baldy Higgins settled in Dry Creek Canyon in the early days when Adam first settled here and when the Sioux was still prowling around.

"He dug himself a hole in the north wall and settled down. He done some trapping, but mostly he lived off what he could kill. In them days we had a lot of game around here. Well, Adam told him two, three times to come here and live on the AP, but he said he was smarter'n any Indian and he'd take care of hisself. He didn't, though. They got his scalp. We found him a week later lying beside the spring."

Sam glared at the old man, anger stirring in him. Then there was a dugout in the canyon, so well covered by the brush and trees that the casual rider would ride past and never notice it. If he and Garber had known about the dugout, they'd have looked for it and might have got Adam out alive.

"Go take care of the horses," Sam said curtly and turned toward the kitchen.

There was no use to go to Dry Creek Canyon now. It would be night before they got there, and it would be so dark in the bottom of the canyon that they wouldn't be able to find the dugout. Besides, it would be guarded, and fumbling around in the darkness trying to find it would be suicide. All they could do was follow instructions and hope that Adam would still be alive tomorrow morning and that Sam would survive Hale's trap—because that was exactly what Hale had set up for him.

Chapter 20

Mike Hale reached the edge of Crow City before it was full dark. Rather than take a chance on being seen, he rode south, circling the town until he reached Crow Creek. He dismounted, watered his horse, and then hunkered beside the stream while he smoked a cigarette.

He heard the whisper of the creek with only half an ear, his thoughts on Tony Arbanz. Slowly the day died and the lamps in Crow City were lighted, the scattered windows looking like pale eyes in the gathering darkness.

In spite of himself, he could not keep his mind on Arbanz and the job he was going to do. It kept turning to the woman who called herself Julie Larkin. She was pretty, she was desirable, and the idea of possessing a woman who belonged to Seth Alexander was so attractive that he promised himself he would pay her a visit before he left town. Once he got her into bed in the hotel room, she wouldn't be so high and mighty.

He was suddenly aware that the last of the daylight was gone. No use putting off a job just because he didn't want to do it, he told himself as he stepped into the saddle. He had killed more men than he could remember, but he had never murdered a defenseless man who was sitting in a chair facing him. It went against his grain.

His father, who had spent more time in jail than out, used to tell him that there was no honor among thieves, that if you didn't look out for yourself, no one else would. Still, he had held to a code of sorts, of never

133

killing a man who didn't have a chance to defend himself. Then he shrugged. He'd told the woman he'd kill Tony Arbanz and he would.

He rode slowly down the creek, turning off on the alley that led to the rear of the business buildings that were located on the south side of Main Street. There was practically no light here, and he rode past the back of Arbanz's print shop before he realized it. He turned, found the right building, and dismounted.

The shop had no rear window, so Hale couldn't tell if Arbanz was still there or not. He felt along the wall until he found the back door, tried it, and discovered that it was unlocked. He gently pushed it open, a patch of yellow lamp light falling into the alley. He stepped into the long room immediately, closing the door quickly. Arbanz was sitting at his desk, writing furiously.

Hale moved toward the editor silently, saying nothing until he was within ten feet of him. Then he said, "You're working late, Tony."

Arbanz jumped and whirled his swivel chair around, saw who it was, and swore. "What the hell are you doing here, Mike?" he demanded, irritated at being interrupted. "And why did you come in through the back? The front door isn't locked."

"I didn't want anyone seeing me come in," Hale said. "I'm going to kill you, so naturally I didn't hanker to have anyone who happened to be walking by see me come in." He moved past Arbanz to the front of the room. "I'd better lock this door, seeing as you say it ain't. I'll pull the blinds, too."

Arbanz's eyes bulged from his head and his mouth sagged open. "You're going to kill me?" he asked, his voice little more than a whisper.

"That's right," Hale said as he locked the street door.

"You're a cold son of a bitch," Arbanz said bitterly. "I figured that Alexander or some of his bunch would do it, but not you."

"It's the same thing," Hale said as he pulled the

blinds down. "He sent the Larkin woman up here to hire me to do it. My day as a law-abiding citizen on the side of the homesteaders is about gone, so I'm taking Alexander's money and leaving Bensen County."

"You're a goddamned liar," Arbanz said, his voice now high and shrill. "Julie Larkin wouldn't do that."

Arbanz started to get up from his chair. Hale had returned to where the editor sat, and he slammed him back into his chair. "I don't know what she told you, but she's Alexander's whore and has been for at least a couple of years. She called herself his housekeeper." He laughed. "You ever hear of a whore wanting to be called a housekeeper?"

Arbanz's face had turned ghastly white. He stared at Hale, his eyes still wide and bulging. "No," he breathed. "It's not true. I . . . I . . ."

"She told me you'd written a book that Alexander wants burned," Hale said, "and he wants you dead so you won't write it over. She said the book was in your desk. Which drawer?"

"It's not here," Arbanz said, his words barely audible. "I took it home."

"I don't believe you," Hale said, "but I'll find out. You sit over yonder next to the wall and stay put while I take a look."

Arbanz didn't move. Hale grabbed him by a shoulder and pulled him to his feet, then gave him a vicious shove in the direction of the chair that sent him sprawling. He struggled to his feet, backed up against the wall, and stood motionless, muttering over and over, "She wouldn't do that to me. She wouldn't."

Hale jerked all the drawers out of the desk and dumped the contents on the floor, but he found nothing that could possibly have been a book. He searched the rest of the office, knocked over the press stand, and kicked a waste basket across the room, but still he found nothing.

"Where is it, Tony?" Hale demanded. "By God, I'll find it if I have to pull your tongue out by the roots."

"It's home," Arbanz whispered. "I told you I took it home. I took it with me last night when I left and worked on it."

Hale chewed on his lower lip, his eyes searching the long room. It wasn't here. Arbanz must be telling the truth. He drew his gun and turned to Arbanz. The editor stood motionless. He had stopped muttering. He had the stoical expression of a man facing his execution. He didn't beg and he didn't run. Hale hesitated, thinking Arbanz was showing a rare form of courage. It was a trait he had seen in a few men and one that he admired.

Hale fired twice, both bullets striking Arbanz in the chest. He was slammed back against the wall, seemed to hang there for an instant, and then his feet slid out from under him and he sprawled full length on the floor. Hale didn't bother to check to see if the editor was dead. People would hear the shots and be swarming around the front of the building in another minute.

Holstering his gun, Hale wheeled and ran out through the back door. He mounted and rode slowly along the alley, not wanting to make any sound that would attract the people who were pounding on the street door. When he reached the creek, he turned downstream and rode under the bridge that spanned the stream. Half a block father down he turned his horse up the bank and into the alley that ran north of Main Street. A minute or so later he reached the rear of the hotel.

The area was not as dark as it had been back of the print shop. One store, he thought it was the drug store, had a lamp in a rear window of the building that laid a patch of yellow lamplight across the dusty alley. Farther on, a lantern hung from a post to light the path between the hotel and the privy.

For a moment Hale hesitated, then decided to ride through the lighted area and leave his horse on the far side of the hotel in a vacant lot between the hotel and the jewelry store, which was just beyond the hotel. He dismounted and, hugging the wall, felt his way back until he reached the rear door. Opening it, he slid inside.

A dimly lighted hall ran the length of the building and led into the lobby. Again Hale hesitated, knowing that the next few seconds would determine his future actions. One thing was in his favor. Only a few minutes had elapsed since he'd left the print shop. The odds were that John Doyle or whoever was at the desk would still be across the street, either pounding on the door of the print shop or standing inside staring at the body.

He strode down the hall as if this were a casual visit. No one was in the lobby or behind the desk. Quickly Hale spun the register, ran his finger down the list of names until he found Julie Larkin's, and noted her room number. Relieved, he wheeled and ran up the stairs. This had been the risky part. If she was in her room, the rest would be easy. If she wasn't, he'd wait.

He found her room, tried the knob, and found that the door was locked. He knocked. A moment later she called, "Who is it?"

"John Doyle," he said. "I thought you'd be interested in hearing what happened across the street."

"No, I don't want to hear about it," she said. "I'm too tired."

He had no time to parley with her, so he stepped back and lunged forward, his shoulder crashing into the door. The flimsy lock snapped and the door flew open. Julie, wearing a nightgown, was sitting up in bed reading. She screamed when the door came open, scrambled out of bed, and ran toward the bureau. Hale caught her before she had covered half the distance and threw her back onto the bed. Turning, he saw that she had been trying to reach her gun on the bureau top.

He shut the door and stood grinning at her. He said, "You ain't so tough now that you don't have your fist on your little pop gun, are you, whore?"

"Get out," she cried. "I told you to tell Doyle to call me. I never wanted to see you again."

"But you are seeing me, smart ass," he said. "The job's done. I want the rest of my money."

She sat on the edge of the bed staring at him. "Where's the book? That was part of the deal."

"There's no book," he said. "I tore Tony's office apart and there wasn't no book there."

"Then you've got all the money you're going to get," she said. "Get out of here before I call Doyle and have you thrown out."

"The day when Doyle can throw me out will be a long time coming." He walked toward the bed, the grin returning to his lips. "I'm going to have the money, and then you'n me are going to have a little get together. When you go back to Alexander, you can tell him you met a real man when you was here."

"The hell we will," she screamed. "I'd as soon get into bed with a snake."

His temper broke then, and he yanked her to her feet and ripped her nightgown as far down as her waist. She bit his hand, drawing blood. He cried out and slapped her across the face. She raised a knee and drove it into his crotch, a hard blow that brought another yelp of pain from him.

His fury rose until he lost all control of himself. He caught her neck between his hands and pressed both thumbs against her throat. She struggled, but the harder she struggled, the harder he squeezed, and then before he realized what he was doing she went limp in his hands.

He threw her back across the bed, only then realizing he had killed her. He stopped and drew a sleeve across his forehead. "My God, woman, I didn't aim to kill you," he muttered, staring at her half-naked body. He had to get out of here. Killing a man was one thing, but killing a woman was something else. They'd lynch him if they found him with her.

Wheeling to her valise, he opened it and dumped the contents on the floor. The second bag of gold was on top of the pile of clothes. He snatched it up, opened the door a crack, and looked along the hall. No one was in sight, but he heard men in the lobby talking in loud tones.

He couldn't get out of the hotel the way he had come in, but there was an outside staircase that led to the alley below. He ran along the hall to the door that opened on the landing at the top of the stairs, stepped outside, and descended the stairs. A moment later he was in the saddle and riding hard out of town.

He didn't slow up until the last light was behind him; then he pulled down to a walk and wiped a hand across his face. It had been close. Too close. He'd played hell for sure. If the damned woman hadn't bitten him and then kicked him in the balls, he wouldn't have lost his temper. He'd have raped her and left her alive. It was her own fault that she was dead, he told himself. But that didn't make any difference. He'd killed her and if Garber or anybody else in town tied him to her death, they'd come after him.

He had almost reached Dry Creek Canyon before he remembered that he had intended to go to the Arbanz house and look for the book. Too late now. A posse might be out looking for him. It wasn't worth it. Anyhow, he had no idea what Alexander would pay for it. Maybe nothing. No, the book wasn't worth it.

Hale knew he was panicky for the first time in his life, but he couldn't help it. He had never killed a woman before. He was sorry. He hadn't intended to kill her. He told himself that over and over. He hadn't intended to kill her, but that wouldn't do any good when they dropped a rope around his neck. They had no way of knowing he did it, but the thought didn't ease the knot that tied up his gut.

A few minutes later he was in the canyon. The Martin boy called out, "Who is it?"

"Mike," he said. "Go on back to sleep."

He rode past where the boy was bedded down in front of the door of the dugout. He offsaddled and staked his horse out far enough from the dugout so that Sam Powers would not be likely to see the animal when he came with the money.

He covered himself with his saddle blanket and tried to sleep, but he could not. The mental picture of Julie Larkin lying dead on the bed kept returning to him, no matter how hard he tried to think of something else.

When the first hint of dawn filtered into the canyon, he woke the Martin boy and said, "Better get up there on the rim, kid. Remember that you're gonna drill Sam Powers as soon as you see him drop the dinero."

The boy yawned and staggered to his feet. "I'll get him," he said in a grumpy tone. "Damned short night."

The boy saddled his horse and rode out through the lower end of the canyon. Hale opened the door of the dugout and looked in, but it was too dark for him to see anything. He called, "You awake, old man?"

Adam didn't say anything for a long moment, then grunted something that was too garbled for Hale to understand. Whatever he'd said didn't make any difference. Hale said, "Won't be long now. Sam will be coming with the money before long and you can walk out of here."

He heard nothing more from Adam. He hunkered down in the doorway as the light deepened with the coming of day. He could see the length of the canyon. All he had to do now was to wait until Sam Powers rode into view.

Hale laughed silently when he thought of young Powers dropping the sack of money, expecting to see his father in a few minutes. Instead, he'd be cut down by the Martin kid's Winchester and the boy would have the satisfaction of beefing his first man.

Hale told himself he'd keep his word to Adam. The old man would walk out of the dugout, all right, but he wouldn't walk far. He laughed again when he considered the cruelty of the joke he was playing on Adam. Then his face turned grave. Not cruel enough, he told himself. Not as cruel as Adam Powers and Seth Alexander and the others had been when they'd surrounded his brother Lon and Bud Larkin and shot them to death.

He had only one regret. He wished that Alexander was here in the dugout with Powers. He wasn't, and Hale had no way of getting at him. Then the thought came to him that by killing Julie Larkin he had gotten at Alexander. For the first time he felt good about killing the woman.

Chapter 21

Sam could not sleep. He lay on his back staring at the black ceiling. He heard coyotes howl from some distant ridge; he heard the creaks and groans of the old house as a sudden gust of wind struck it. Once he sat up, thinking he heard someone ride by, and then lay back, knowing it was his imagination.

He and Bronc had agreed to leave at three, deciding that a two-hour ride would bring them to Dry Creek Canyon before sunup. The minutes dragged by, and he was shocked when he heard the downstairs clock strike twelve. He thought it was long after midnight, that it was almost time to leave.

Normally he fell asleep the instant he got into bed, but there had never been another night in his life like this. One thing that kept him awake was Betty's presence in the next room. In a few days she would be in bed beside him. It could have been tonight, he told himself.

Waiting had been hard on both of them, but he thought it had been worse for him because part of Betty's mind had been fastened on her father and his

141

problems, and she could not free herself from those problems.

He had been surprised, then, when she had clung to him outside her bedroom after they had climbed the stairs, and even more surprised when she had thrown her head back and looked up at him, a faint smile on her lips.

"You'll think I'm as wicked as the Larkin woman," she said softly, "but I've waited too long for you. I don't want to wait any longer."

Surprised, he said, "I'd never think you was anything like the Larkin woman, but I'm remembering what you said about it not doing me any good to be sleeping in the room next to yours."

The smile left her lips. She looked at him, her lips quivering, then she brought his face down to hers and kissed him, her lips soft and inviting. "I know," she said. "How well I know. I wished I hadn't said it as soon as the words were out of my mouth. I got to thinking about it. Suppose you're killed in the morning?"

"I won't be," he said. "Bronc and me figgered it out." He shook his head sadly. "Honey, you know there's nothing in the whole, big world I'd rather do than go into your room with you. I'd do it if we were alone at your place, but Bronc's sleeping in the other upstairs bedroom and he's a light sleeper. Ma would guess, too. She's got a way of knowing about things like that."

She released her grip and stepped back, smiling again. "I guess I couldn't have gone through with it, Sam. It's just that I want you so much. I've been happier since I met you than I'd ever been before in my life. I know it's terrible for me to say this, but I don't really care one way or the other about Adam. For you to lose your life trying to save his is . . ."

A sob shook her body and she whirled, opened the door to her room, and ran through it, shutting the door hard behind her. He stood staring at the door, regretting what he'd said. He wouldn't have said it if he'd had time to think. To hell with what Bronc thought. Or his mother, either.

Now, lying in bed with the darkness pressing against him, he regretted it more than ever. He simply had not had the courage to accept the gift she had offered, to do what he wanted to do and what she had wanted him to do.

Again he thought, as he had so many times these last days, that giving his life in an effort to save Adam's was a poor bargain any way he looked at it. Yet that was the way it might go. He was not his own man; he could not change the decision he had made. Right or wrong, he was committed.

He dropped off to sleep. It seemed that only a few seconds had passed when a tap on his door woke him. He sat up, a terrible fear that he had overslept paralyzing him.

"What is it?" he called.

"The sheriff's here," his mother said. "He wants to see you and Bronc."

"I'll be right down," he said, so shocked by what she had said that he wondered if he had misunderstood her, and knew immediately that he had not.

He lit a lamp and dressed, a dozen explanations surging through his mind for Garber's coming to the AP at this hour. None of them made any sense. Garber didn't even know about the ransom note. Sam hadn't thought the lawman would go with him and Bronc to Dry Creek Canyon, so he hadn't told him about the note. He'd already had more help from Garber than he had expected.

When he stepped out of his room into the hall, he saw that Betty's door was ajar and she was staring at him. She asked in a low, frightened tone, "What is it, Sam?"

"I don't rightly know," he answered. "Ma just told me that Ed Garber's here. I'm going to see what he wants."

He walked quickly past her, afraid that if he stopped

143

to kiss her, or even to talk to her, he wouldn't be able to leave. As he went down the stairs he wondered bitterly if any man had ever been caught in a trap like this before, wanting something so much and knowing he could not have it at this time.

Ed Garber was waiting in the living room. He tried to grin, but it turned into a grimace. "I ain't sure I'm doing right, waking you up in the middle of the night, but some things have been happening that I thought you'd want to know about. Mostly it's a matter of being worried about Miss Arbanz. I stopped at her place, but I couldn't raise anybody."

"She's spending the night here," Sam said. "We were worried about her, too, so we persuaded her to stay with us."

"I've put the coffee pot on," Ida Powers said from the kitchen doorway. "Why don't you come and sit down at the table? The coffee'll be ready in a minute."

Bronc came clumping down the stairs, rubbing his eyes as if he couldn't pry them open. Sam glanced at the wall clock. It was nearly three. He had thought it was later. He jerked his head toward the kitchen and led the way, Garber and Bronc following.

"There's hell to pay," Garber said. "I figger Hale's our man, but I don't have nothing to go on. It's just that he's the worst outlaw in the county and I keep thinking about him ever since we was out there." He swallowed, then added, "Tony Arbanz was shot and killed tonight."

Sam stiffened, staring at the sheriff, so shocked that for a moment he couldn't fully grasp what he'd heard. His thoughts and fears had been fastened on his own father, and as far as he knew, Betty's worries about Tony were concerned only with his getting into bed with Julie Larkin.

Ida Powers cried out, an incoherent sound as if this, the last in a series of unhappy events, was too much. Bronc swore, and Garber added, "I guess you folks can notify his daughter."

"We'll tell her," Sam said, and could not think of

anything that he dreaded more. "When did it happen?"

"I ain't real sure," Garber said. "I didn't hear the shots. I was home, but several men who were on Main Street, including John Doyle, who was standing in front of his hotel, heard 'em. They tried the front door of his print shop, but it was locked. They finally broke it down when they pounded on it and he didn't answer. He was dead when they found him. The place was all tore up, like somebody was looking for something. It was close to ten when I got there. All I know is that he was killed before that."

Sam sipped his coffee, turning this over in his mind. He didn't know what motive Hale would have, but he agreed with Garber that Hale was the worst man in the county, capable of doing anything. But even Hale had to have a reason.

Finally Sam asked, "Why?"

"Dunno," Garber said. "I don't even have a guess, but that ain't all. Julie Larkin was murdered in her room a few minutes later."

Sam was more shocked by this killing than he was by Arbanz's murder. It was reasonable to guess that Arbanz had been killed by someone hired by Alexander and his friends and that the shop had been ransacked in an effort to find the book Tony Arbanz had written, but why Hale would be involved puzzled him. As far as the Larkin woman's killing was concerned, he couldn't see any connection with Arbanz's death or any motive for it.

"You think there's a connection between the two killings?" Sam asked.

"Probably," Garber answered, "but I don't savvy what it is, and I don't savvy why Hale would do it, if he did kill Arbanz. All I know is that they must have happened a few minutes apart, long enough for Hale to go to the hotel from the print shop, and at a time when anybody who was in the hotel would have gone over to see what the shooting was about.

"Doyle found her body. She'd been strangled. Her suitcase had been upended and her clothes were piled up on the floor, so whoever done it was looking for something, same as in the print shop. Doyle called Doc, and Doc said she'd been killed a little while before he got there."

Ida Powers had been weeping quietly. Now she said in a low tone, "I'm not shedding any tears for the Larkin woman, but I am for Betty. The loss of her father will be a hard blow to her."

"I figgered it would be," Garber said. "Tony was a hothead, always stirring things up. He would have strung your husband up if he'd got his hands on him, but in most ways he was a decent man."

He finished his coffee and cleared his throat. "Sam, there's something else that might be important to you on account of your pa. Art Palmer and the Larkin woman came to my office late in the afternoon, saying they'd been riding through Dry Creek Canyon, when she stopped to get a drink. Somebody shot at 'em from the north rim. Palmer ain't one to get boogered real easy, but he was still scared when he talked to me. He said there was just one shot that was meant to scare 'em, so they got out of the canyon in a hurry. What do you make of that?"

Sam glanced at Bronc, who nodded somberly. He was feeling guilty for not thinking of the dugout sooner, Sam thought, and he ought to be.

"I'd say there was something in the canyon that somebody don't want found." He rose. "We'd better go see what it is."

"I'll go along," Garber said. "I'm a little curious myself."

"We can use you," Sam said, and nodded at his mother. "Let Betty sleep. Telling her now won't change anything."

Ida nodded. "I'll wait."

Sam studied the sheriff for a moment. "I don't get it, Ed," he said. "I had a hell of a time getting you to go after Hale with me. Now you're wanting to go. What got into you?"

Garber stared at the floor, his face turning red. "Don't make much sense, I reckon, but after it was over, it felt damned good to be doing what I knew I oughtta do." He looked up and added defiantly, "Now I want to finish the job."

"That's what we're gonna do," Sam said.

He went into the front room, took his gun belt off the antler rack near the door, and buckled it around him. He picked up the sack of newspaper he had cut into rectangles the size of greenbacks the night before, lighted a lantern, then reached for his Winchester.

As he turned to the door and opened it, he glanced at his mother, who was standing in the center of the room watching him. She wasn't crying now, but he sensed what she was thinking.

He said, "I'll be back," and went out into the night, Bronc and Garber following him.

Chapter 22

They rode south across the grass. There was no north–south road in this part of the county, so Sam, who was in the lead, took as direct a course as he could across the dry washes and around occasional rock outcroppings, but it took longer to reach Dry Creek Canyon than he had anticipated. The eastern sky was showing color by the time they reached the west end of the canyon, but sunup was still a quarter of an hour or more away.

Garber had asked about the sack that Sam was carrying. When Sam told him about the note, the sheriff said, "That explains what I was only suspicioning, but I ain't sure you're going to fool whoever's on the rim. You may get knocked off the minute you drop the sack."

"I thought of that," Sam admitted. "I figger I've got to stay close to the north wall; then maybe the man on the rim won't get a good bead on me."

"I've got a better idea," Garber said. "Me'n Bronc could flush the drygulcher out before you drop the sack."

"And get yourself killed," Sam said.

"It's what I'm paid for," Garber said, "and I'm guessing Bronc ain't worried about dying, seeing as he's lived twice as long as either one of us."

"Hell no," Bronc said sarcastically. "I ain't worrying about dying. I'm downright anxious to see old St. Peter standing at the pearly gate so I can shake his hand."

"I'll do the job myself, then," Garber said sharply.

"I never seen a man change so much," Sam said. "I still don't savvy."

"I think we can do the job without getting ourselves rubbed out," Garber said. "It ain't that I want to shake St. Peter's hand no more'n Bronc does. Just makes sense that Hale's set a trap for you. Chances are he's already killed your pa and he's waiting to give you the same medicine to get you off his back."

"All right, we'll play it your way," Sam said. "What do you think, Bronc?"

"Oh, Ed here might get lonesome if I don't keep him company," Bronc said.

Now, with the opalescent light of dawn slowly spreading across the prairie, Sam reined up. He asked, "Still want to go ahead?"

"Sure," Garber answered. "We'll leave our horses yonder in the gully and crawl up on him. Give us fifteen minutes before you go sashaying into the canyon."

"That should do it," Sam said, and turned his horse down the steep slope.

As Sam slowly descended into the canyon, the thought struck him that Garber was trying to make up for his dereliction of duty. Or perhaps he had been living with a guilty conscience from the time he had been elected. Either way, Sam was glad to have an ace in the hole he had not planned on when he had first discussed the problem with Bronc.

They had intended to ride into the canyon, hoping to stay close enough to the base of the north rim to avoid being seen by the ambusher on top. There was enough overhang so that he thought it would work, but he couldn't picture the north cliff well enough to be sure, and he'd had a terrible feeling that they might be sitting ducks for anyone who was waiting on the rim for them and was an average marksman.

Garber's plan was better. The chances were that the man on the rim would be hunkered down, or lying flat on his belly among the rocks, his eyes on the bottom of the canyon, and he would not expect anyone to be stalking him.

When Sam reached the canyon bottom, he found that the shadows had lingered here, so that the visibility was poor, certainly not clear enough for accurate shooting from the rim. He estimated that he had used up less than ten minutes reaching the bottom of the canyon. Sunup was now several minutes away. Still, the chances that he would survive were better than they would be a few minutes later, when the light would have deepened.

He reined up, crowding the north wall, and considered the murky light around him, the tall cottonwoods ghostly in the shadows. Better take the chance now, he decided. He rode forward for another twenty yards, then turned sharply away from the wall and shouted, "Here's your dinero," as he dropped the sack.

He had not thought the situation would explode as suddenly as it did. Instantly a man on the rim began firing, bullets snapping past him to strike the tree trunks to the south or bury themselves in the dirt on the opposite wall of the canyon.

Sam flung himself off his horse and dived back toward the north wall, as other guns on the rim began adding to the explosion of sound. Suddenly he saw a man stagger into the open, as if he had erupted out of the solid north wall. The light was still too thin to see the man clearly at this distance, but he realized that the man was reeling as violently as a willow caught in the wind. He was suffering either from weakness of body or the feebleness of old age.

Sam's first impulse was to shoot because he still couldn't identify the man. He thought it might be some kind of weird trick that only Hale would think of, that the outlaw was trying to get closer to be sure he hit his target. But before Sam pulled the trigger of his Winchester, he realized that it might be his father, perhaps escaping from the dugout for the first time since it had become his prison.

Sam ran forward, calling, "Pa," but before he had gone ten feet, he heard a shot from directly ahead of him. The reeling man threw up his hands and toppled forward on his face. Behind him was the vague figure of a man, half-hidden in the dugout door. He had stepped out only far enough to shoot the fugitive. Sam fired, having less than half a man for his target, but it was enough. His slug knocked the man off his feet and brought him tumbling out of the dugout.

It had to be Hale, Sam thought as he ran forward, although he had not seen enough to be sure. The outlaw rolled over and sat up, and began firing with his Colt. The first shot was the only real chance he had and he missed. His next shot was wild and that was his last. Sam's second bullet drove through his chest, and he dropped flat into the dirt and gravel of the canyon bottom, his gun spinning out of his hand.

Sam continued to move forward, slowly and carefully now, still holding his rifle on the ready. He passed his father, suspecting that Hale was playing possum, but when he reached the man, he saw that he was hard hit. He knelt beside him, asking, "Why did you kill Tony Arbanz?"

"The Larkin woman hired me to kill him for

Alexander," he whispered. "Now go to hell and let me die."

"Then why kill the Larkin woman?"

"I didn't aim to," he breathed. "She wouldn't give me my dinero, so . . . I . . ."

That was all. Sam rose and wheeled away from him, certain that there was no more evil in this man who had done so much harm in the last few days. Sam stood looking down at his father, who was barely alive, shocked by the old man's thin, chalky face, by the smell that rose from his body, by the filth that covered his clothes.

"Pa," Sam said as he knelt in the gravel beside his father.

Adam's eyes flickered open. He said, "Sam," in a whisper so soft that Sam wouldn't have heard if he hadn't leaned down so he was close to his father's mouth. "I wouldn't have blamed you if you hadn't come for me." He stopped, blood bubbling on his lips, and Sam thought he had stopped breathing, but he still had enough life to say, "The bastard told me you was here and I was free to go. I should have known what he'd do."

He died then, lying in the dust a few feet from the man who had killed him. Sam rose and for a long moment stared down at this lump of clay that had been his father. The thought that the imperious, domineering man he had known as Adam Powers could have been reduced to something less than a man, something filthy and ugly, something without dignity, was more than he could bear.

Sam turned away, sick at his stomach. He saw Hale's horse tied in the brush fifty yards down the canyon. He brought the animal to where Adam's body lay and tied him across the saddle. He hesitated, staring at the open door of the dugout that had been Adam's prison, thinking that incarceration in that black hole would be enough to destroy any man.

He walked to the dugout and stepped inside, the

151

stink hitting him with the force of a tangible blow. He backed through the door into the sunlight that had just now touched the bottom of the canyon, his gaze taking in the dirty bunk, the stove, the candle on the table, the plate of food, and the cup of coffee.

Wheeling, he kicked Hale's body and swore. "You son of a bitch," he said angrily. "You got even for Lon's death and then some."

Taking the reins of Hale's horse, Sam led the animal to where he had left his own mount. Garber was descending the north slope of the canyon just west of where it became a sheer wall of rock, a cloud of dust rising behind him.

"What happened?" Garber asked when he reached Sam. "We heard a shot just as we were ready to move in on the Martin kid. That's who was up there."

"I reckon I jumped the gun by a minute or two," Sam said. "I started the ball because I figured that he couldn't hit me with the light as pale as it was." He looked at Garber and shook his head. "I guess I just couldn't wait any longer."

"We were a mite worried," Garber said. "We didn't spot the kid for a while until he started shooting; then we saw where he was hunkered down in a rockpile on the rim, and it took us a little longer to get to him than we figgered on." He paused, glanced at Adam's body, and asked, "Hale?"

"Dead," Sam said. "He shot Pa just before I got him. I figure that when he heard the shooting from the rim, he thought the kid had plugged me, so he shoved Pa through the door. That was his mistake."

"I'm glad it's over," Garber said. "I can start breathing again. I've been scared, Sam. By God, I've never been so scared in my life, but I'll tell you one thing. I'm going to be sheriff from now on. I found out something about myself." As Sam stepped into the saddle, Garber asked, "Think we oughtta bury Hale and go after Martin?"

Sam shook his head. "Martin can bury his partner. I

can't blame Martin for what happened. It was Hale all the way. Is the kid dead?"

"No, we just winged him," Garber answered. "I sent Bronc into town with him to see the doc. You going home?"

"I'm going home," Sam said, and started riding west out of the canyon.

"I'll go along," Garber said. "Miss Arbanz may want to talk to me."

"I figger she will," Sam said.

Strange, Sam told himself, that his father and Betty's father should be killed within a few hours of each other. Although they had been killed by the same man, the reasons for the killings were entirely different. A new life was opening up, a new life for Betty and him, and for Bensen County, the invasion finally behind them. Now homesteaders and townspeople could look forward and not backward.

A Special Preview of
the blazing opening section of
the first novel in the new series
A Saga of the Southwest

THE HAWK
AND THE
DOVE
by
Leigh Franklin James

A Saga of the Southwest will trace the trials
and triumphs of a group of hardy people from
diverse backgrounds who endure hardships while
trying to build a dazzling dynasty in the Southwest.

Martin snorted. "You was born to hate, Mike. You

1

Now John Cooper could see a thin plume of smoke rising from the chimney of the cabin. He figured that his mother had started a fire for supper and anticipated her happiness when he presented her with two fine ducks for roasting. They'd go mighty fine with sweet yams. Hopefully she'd bake a pie tomorrow from the berries.

They had come now to a cornfield, some two hundred yards behind the cabin. There had been enough rain and heat this summer to produce a bountiful crop, and the tassled stalks rose as high as John Cooper's head. His father had already sent a dozen bushels to the village of Pesquetaba, chief of the Shawnee, and would doubtless send more before the season was over.

John Cooper knew that his father made whiskey from some of the corn, using the formula which his father had taught him back in Ireland. Sometimes, Andrew Baines sold jugs of whiskey to neighbors or visiting trappers. But when he first settled in Shawneetown, Andrew had told old Pesquetaba that this drink was only for the sick and the dying. And Pesquetaba seemed to accept the white lie. Andrew had explained to his son that it was both dangerous and illegal to sell whiskey to Indians.

John Cooper was about to skirt the cornfield and head for the cabin when he suddenly froze. The sounds of shots and angry cries reached him. Lije pricked up his ears and growled softly. "Quiet, Lije!" John Cooper snapped in a hoarse whisper. He had gone very pale, and his eyes were fixed with disbelief on the scene beyond him.

There were at least ten of them, Shawnee braves, their heads shaved bare save for the scalplock, naked except for buckskin leggings, breechclouts, and moccasins. One of them lay sprawled near the door of the cabin. Even as John Cooper stared, a musket shot sounded from inside the cabin and another brave dropped his tomahawk, clutched his belly, and rolled over and over on the ground in his death agonies.

"Oh, sweet Jesus . . . oh, no . . . oh, God . . . they're after ma and pa and Elsie and Ginny!" the boy gasped. "I haven't even got any birdshot left in my musket. . . . Quick, Lije, into the corn, before they see us!" Still holding the berry-filled hat, he bolted into the thick cornstalks. The wolfhound followed, with another low growl which drew a warning "Shhh!" from the agonized boy.

Inching forward on his belly to the last rows of corn, John Cooper peered through the stalks while Lije obediently lay down beside him, still gripping the musket. Two of the braves had brought along a cedar log and were now battering the door of the cabin. One of them, from behind the high stump of an oak tree, was reloading an old long rifle. He took careful aim at the shuttered window of the cabin and fired. John Cooper could hear a faint cry from inside. He clenched his teeth, tears nearly blinding him. "What am I going to do? How can I help them in there? All I've got is my hunting knife. . . . They've got tomahawks and muskets and that old rifle. Oh please, dear sweet God, don't let them hurt ma and pa and the girls—I swear I won't ever lie again or shirk my chores and lessons if you'll just save 'em, Lord, please!"

Once again he heard the sharp bark of his father's rifle. One of the braves, who had been loping toward the back of the cabin, stopped in his tracks, then toppled like an ax-felled oak. But two more braves had joined their companions with the battering log. Drawing back and using all their strength, they crashed through the door with hideous whoops.

"Why, why?" John Cooper groaned as he turned to stare at the wolfhound. "We never did the Shawnee

any harm. They've been friends ever since we got here."
The wolfhound stared back at him, his eyes angry and
bright, still gripping the musket barrel between his jaws.

John Cooper stifled a cry of horror. Two of the
braves had dragged his father out, and the Shawnee
who had been crouching behind the stump flung down
his rifle and ran forward, brandishing a tomahawk. As
Andrew Baines struggled frantically, the tomahawk
descended. John Cooper closed his eyes and bit his lips
until they bled to control the shout of rage and horror
which rose within him. The two braves who had been
holding his father let the lifeless body fall and rushed
into the cabin with the others.

Now John Cooper could hear screams and tearful
pleas. He forced himself to look, trembling violently.
One brave dragged out his gentle mother, her sweet,
heart-shaped face contorted in agony at the sight of her
murdered husband. "Oh, Andrew . . . why have you
done this to him? Don't harm the girls . . . take me!"

Two braves ripped her homespun dress from her
and then her underclothing. They flung her, naked, down
on the ground. John Cooper buried his tear-drenched
face in the earth and groaned aloud. He could hear his
mother's sobs and groans as a young brave brutally and
vigorously ravished her while two of his companions
held her down on the bloodstained ground, near her
husband's body.

By the time her fourth assailant had finished with
her, she lay, moaning feebly, her face twisted to one
side. The man who had her last, the oldest of them,
seized the musket she had used inside the cabin to defend her brood and, swinging it by the barrel, dashed
out her brains with a triumphant bellow.

Now the others dragged out John Cooper's sisters
—thirteen-year-old Elsie, and Virginia, three years
older. Seeing her parents lying dead, Elsie broke away
from her captors, flung herself to her knees and hys-
terically begged them not to die and leave her. The
Shawnee hooted at her childlike pathos, one of them
twisting his fingers into her long, golden curls and
dragging her out toward the stump, while two others

followed. The other four amused themselves with Virginia, who fought them with her fingernails and desperate kicks . . . but all in vain.

John Cooper had retched. Now his body still shaking, he watched the hideous aftermath of this inexplicable attack by these braves, many of whom he had known since his family's arrival in Shawneetown. Lije growled again, and the agonized boy put his hand to the dog's nose and shook his head. Then he watched until he could look no more. His sisters were violently ravished, and then they, too, were tomahawked.

The triumphant marauders rushed into the cabin. A few minutes later, three of them emerged carrying clay jugs of Andrew Baines's whiskey. Chanting and boasting, they passed the jugs among themselves until they were empty.

The sun had already set, and a gentle twilight bathed the cornfield and the cabin. John Cooper could hear the placid gurgling of the broad Ohio River as it flowed southward to meet the mighty Mississippi. Night birds began to twitter, but their sounds were drowned out by the Shawnee's boisterous, drunken bursts of laughter.

The boy waited helplessly for what seemed like an eternity. He was violently sick from what he had seen, torn asunder by his all-consuming grief and rage. Almost mechanically, he reached for his musket, and Lije obediently opened his mouth. John Cooper sobbed softly as he flung the useless weapon away, and the ducks with it. "Now quiet, we've got to wait until they go away, Lije," he muttered thickly.

The silver quarter of the moon had risen by the time the Shawnee began to stumble to their feet and move northwestward, back to their camp. Only two remained, a young warrior John Cooper knew, and the oldest brave, who had been last with Ruth Cooper Baines. They lay in a drunken stupor, the young Indian, Nisquah, clutching the barrel of Andrew Baines's Lancaster.

All was still now. The night birds called insistently to one another, and there was the sound of the water lapping. John Cooper could hear the croaking of a bull-frog as he got to his feet slowly, again putting his hand to Lije's muzzle to keep the dog quiet. He moved swiftly toward the cabin, trying not to look at the bodies of his murdered family. His eyes burned with tears and his throat was raw with unuttered shouts and curses. For a moment he stood staring down at the older brave, who was muttering in his drunken stupor. He saw the bloody tomahawk which had murdered his father, seized it, knelt down and, lifting it, smashed it with all his strength first against Nisquah's skull. Then he whirled swiftly and raised the tomahawk again to avenge his mother.

He left the tomahawk buried in the older brave's skull as he walked into the cabin. Lije uttered a low, angry whine as he saw the bodies of those whose protector and friend he had been since first Andrew Baines had carried him in a sling aboard the ship bound for America.

John Cooper came out with a spade and began to dig four graves. He sobbed while he worked. Gently, John Cooper lowered his father into the first grave and covered him. Tears were streaming down his face. "Oh God, if only I hadn't gone hunting today," he muttered when it was done.

Then, reverently, having brought out sheets from their bedding to cover the naked bodies of his mother and sisters, he lowered gentle Ruth Cooper to her final resting place. How kind, how good she had always been to him and how he had loved her. He remembered bolting down all those blackberries. "If you'd seen me, ma, you'd have scolded me good and proper. You always taught me to eat slowly. . . . I'll not forget it, not ever." He broke down, covering his face with his hands, his wiry, young body shuddering violently.

He rose again and forced himself to bury Virginia. How often his big sister had teased him—she used to say that it was a shame he hadn't been born a hunting dog like Lije, so that he could spend all his time in the woods.

Again he got to his feet, drying his swollen eyes with the sleeve of his jacket. His mother had sewn it for him. There was something he had to do for little Elsie. He'd really brought back the blackberries for her—she loved them best. He remembered how she'd asked him to whittle toys and dolls for her. He hurried back to the cornfield. Stooping down, he retrieved the berry-filled hat and returned to the last grave, in which he had laid his younger sister. Kneeling down, he put the hat on her bosom and then, with an agonized sob, began to cover her.

The earth would be gentle with them, he knew— gentler than those damned Shawnee had been. But why had they killed his family? What he didn't, couldn't know was that they had turned renegade and defied Pesquetaba's order. They'd murdered old Henry Dolson, who lived about a mile downriver, and found two jugs of whiskey in his cabin. Putting two and two together because of Baines's big cornfield, they'd come back to demand whiskey from Andrew Baines and he'd refused them.

"What do we do now, Lije?" John Cooper turned to the wolfhound, his voice hollow and despondent. "There's nothing left for me here any more. Maybe we'll go west. I sure don't want to go to Indiana to see cousin Matthew and his Shawnee wife. . . . I don't want to think about Shawnee, ever again. Besides, he's got his life and his kids, and we'd just be in the way. So we'll go west. First, though, we've got to get some provisions. I'll take pa's Lancaster and his powder horn, lead and bullet mold, and all the balls he's got left. We might need all that if we run across hostiles on the trail."

He went into the cabin, his head bowed, his body slumped in despair. Lije followed hesitantly, silent and observing as John Cooper packed the supplies necessary for the journey.

Outside the cabin once again, John Cooper tugged Andrew Baines's Lancaster from Nisquah's stiffening hand. Then he headed toward the bank of the river, Lije at his heels.

"We'll get on pa's log raft, and float ourselves down the Ohio to a likely spot, then cross over and head out west," he thought to himself.

Setting the heavy sack down on the raft, he shoved it toward the water's edge, remembering to take the long pole used for steering. Then, nimbly leaping aboard, he whistled to Lije, who leaped swiftly onto the raft and stood wagging his tail, looking up at his young master.

"You're all I've got left now, Lije. We'll see each other through this. God'll take care of us. Maybe someday I'll turn out to be the gentleman ma always wanted me to be. Let's go now." John Cooper's voice had steadied. It was as if he were standing off to one side, hearing himself talk to the wolfhound. He felt drained, exhausted. He willed himself with all his waning strength to push from his mind what he had been forced to watch.

He heard the croak of a bullfrog as he shoved the raft out into the gently flowing waters of the Ohio. He did not look back at the cabin, receding in the distance, now dark, with only the silver of the moon in a cloudless sky to illuminate his forever abandoned boyhood home.

2

"If you will wait here, Don Diego, His Majesty will see you presently. He has matters of state requiring his immediate attention, you understand." The majordomo, resplendent in his red brocade coat and powdered wig, grasped his staff of office and gave the gray-haired nobleman a peremptory nod. Then, turning stiffly, he walked away, leaving Don Diego de Escobar alone in the great hall to await his private audience with His Most Catholic Majesty, Charles IV.

The night before, a royal courier had brought a summons to Don Diego's estate on the outskirts of Madrid, commanding him to present himself to the king this dreary September morning. The impersonal brevity of that summons had puzzled Don Diego. He, and his father before him, had served the Spanish crown with honor and dignity. Now as he stood gazing at the portrait of Philip II, painted by Juan Pantoja de la Cruz, he tried to compose his thoughts and prepare himself for this unexpected audience.

Don Diego de Escobar, forty-seven years old, was a man of medium height and stately bearing. His goatee and mustache were silver gray, and he disdained the formal wig. His head was leonine and his hair, though as gray as his goatee and mustache, was thick and full and showed no sign of thinning with his advancing age. He glanced back at the retreating figure of the majordomo and smiled wryly to himself. There, indeed, was a man who had need of a wig. Under it, the Count Pedro de Santorsalva was as bald as an egg.

He stared up again at the portrait, reflecting that the Escorial represented all the glory that was royal

Spain. Built in a twenty-one-year period during the reign of Philip II, it included a massive palace, a monastery, and a church; and it housed the tombs of Spain's greatest monarchs. Everywhere one saw the decorations of great artists, and its library and collection of Spanish paintings were world-renowned. From this place, gloomy and dark with its centuries-old secrets, the man whom de la Cruz had so vividly immortalized with oils on canvas had brought Spain to its very zenith of colonization and prosperity.

Don Diego de Escobar could not turn his gaze from that portrait. He saw the heavy-lidded eyes, cold and merciless, the thin lips, the hand that clutched orb and scepter, and the other that was flung out contemptuously toward a map of the then-known world. He had, of course, seen other great portraits of this indomitable Philip—the ones by Titian, A. Coello, and the more familiar portrait by this same de la Cruz, which showed the king in full armor. Yet this was the one which always held his attention. The painter had captured the autocratic sovereignty which Philip II had so gloriously exemplified.

Don Diego sighed nostalgically. There had been a de Escobar, a young captain out of Seville, who had commanded a troop of arquebusiers during Philip's religious invasion of the Netherlands. Indeed, all of his descendants since then had served the king with joy and honor. The very father of the monarch whom he now awaited had bestowed the title of nobility on Carlos de Escobar, Don Diego's father. And he, Don Diego, had named his only son Carlos, after both monarchs, in gratitude for that honor.

At last he turned away from the imposing portrait to stare at the door of the antechamber in which he would be received when it pleased his royal master. The thought of his son, now sixteen, and of his lovely willful daughter, Catarina, three years younger, brought sharply back to mind his deep concern over their mother's illness. Dolores de Escobar, his handsome, thirty-five-year-old wife, had been suffering from a strange fever for more than a month. Her spinster sister, two years older, Doña Inez de Castillana, had come to Madrid to nurse her and help care for the household and the children. When Don Diego had received the royal summons, he had said nothing of it to Dolores or Inez; there was no need to worry either of them. But he felt uneasy—he couldn't understand why he had been summoned so urgently.

Almost unconsciouly, Don Diego de Escobar straightened his shoulders. He remembered with pride how the king had invited him, last February, to inspect the royal bodyguard at the Escorial. He had walked down the line of brilliantly caparisoned soldiers, their cabassets glittering under the rays of the cold morning sun, their boots immaculately polished, their muskets gripped tightly at salute. Charles IV had turned to him and said, "Don Diego, men like these truly inspire one to be a king, *¿no es verdad?*" Don Diego had smiled and inclined his head as he replied, "As they do me to be your most loyal subject, my king."

Yet now, remembering that moment, Don Diego was saddened by his own misgivings. If only Charles IV had shown the same forthrightness as his illustrious father. But instead, dominated by his queen, the dissolute Maria Louisa of Parma, and her lover Manuel de Godoy—whom he had made his chief minsiter in 1792—the fifty-nine-year-old monarch was weak and vacillating in this hour of Spain's greatest need.

Don Diego de Escobar had disliked Manuel de Godoy from the very first. Cunning and unscrupulous and even two-faced, he had first favored war on revolutionary France. Then, for some reason, he quickly changed and advocated peace instead. In Don Diego's opinion, if war had been declared, the threat of Napoleon would never have arisen. But Godoy had negotiated a peace in 1795 and, since then, seemed to side with the French on all issues, even those which would affect Spanish territory.

Gradually the colonies of Spain's glorious New World were being undermined by the king's own vacillation and his prime minister's treacherous loyalty to the French. To a *Madrileño* like Don Diego, it was a desperately trying situation, one which struck at his own devotion to his native land and his oath of allegiance to the monarch whom he now anxiously awaited.

Suddenly he heard the reedy voice of Count Pedro de Santorsalva, the majordomo. "His Majesty will see you now, Don Diego. Follow me, *por favor.*"

Don Diego de Escobar drew a deep breath and turned to the majordomo. His thoughts had led him to a conclusion—he would be forthright with Charles IV. Of course, he would not dare slander the royal household by alluding to Godoy. That would serve only to remind the king of his own complacence in the face of cuckoldry. But he would urge Charles IV to strengthen the troops that guarded the peninsular boundaries. Despite the pact with France, he did not trust Napoleon. History had already shown the Corsican's greed and overwhelming ambition. If that mighty army moved against Spain—as it had against Austria, Russia, and Sweden—then Philip II's valor and all the glory of the Escorial would become mere legend.

Don Diego followed the count down a narrow corridor. He waited while the latter struck three times with his staff upon the floor and then almost reverently opened the door, bowing low as he announced, "Don Diego de Escobar, as you have bidden, *vuestro Majestad.*"

The count moved away and hurried back down the corridor as Don Diego entered the floridly decorated antechamber, carefully closing the door behind him. He went down on one knee, pressing a fervent kiss upon the limp, fat hand of Charles IV. As he rose to his feet, he declared, "I await your orders, my king."

Charles IV was portly. He wore a white wig and a jeweled sword hung at his side. His round face was mottled, his lip trembled, and he showed already the malady of dropsy which was to afflict him sorely. He turned toward the velvet-curtained window, his back to Don Diego, and spoke in a querulous voice. "I fear the orders I have concerning you, Don Diego, will not be to your liking."

"In what way have I failed Your Majesty?" Don Diego stood stiffly, arms at his sides, head erect—but he was consumed by an uneasy premonition.

The king turned back to his writing desk, drew out the cherrywood chair before it, and sat down. Covering his mouth, he uttered a soft belch. He scowled, staring at the documents awaiting his signature. Then, again without looking at Don Diego, he went on, "My consort and my chief minister have asked that I punish you for treason, Don Diego."

"Treason? Your Majesty!" The gray-haired nobleman was aghast. "But surely you must know, my king, that my father and I have devoted our lives to the throne and that we are the most loyal Spaniards in your realm."

"That is what I argued, Don Diego." At last Charles IV deigned to look up at him. Don Diego perceived an almost pathetic expression in the king's watery eyes and twitching lips. "Indeed, had I not convinced them that you and your illustrious father had done much for the throne, I should be disconsolate at passing on to you their judgment."

"Judgment, my king?" Don Diego's voice quivered.

"Did you not say to the Count Jorge de Murciano that you believed it to be a fatal blunder of statemanship to ally Spain with France?"

Don Diego de Escobar closed his eyes and shuddered. He remembered all too well that chance remark. Yet it had been taken out of context by Murciano, who, he knew, had long envied him his rank in court and the high esteem he had hitherto enjoyed. Yes, now it was all too terribly clear.

"But Your Majesty, that was not all I said. I do not know how it was that our casual conversation came to the ears of Queen Maria Louisa and Prime Minister Godoy, but I assure you that there was nothing traitorous in the implication. What I said—if I may be permitted to recall it to your Majesty—was that Spain has always gained strength from its colonies in the New World, and that I feared only that preoccupation with French affairs would endanger our control of those colonies. Even if we are at peace with France, surely

Your Majesty must realize that Napoleon would scrap a treaty in a minute if it suited his purpose. Even now he is devising a campaign that will tear us asunder and strip us as a world power, all the while pretending to maintain peace. Do you believe that statement to be traitorous, my king?"

Charles IV made an ineffectual gesture with one fat hand, as if brushing away the argument. Finally, he cleared his throat. "The unalterable fact, Don Diego, is that you have placed me in an untenable position. Her Royal Majesty Maria Louisa believes that a subject who does not concur with our statesmanship should not be attached to the royal court. Yes, I well know how you and your father have served Spain! Yet I must accede to the wishes of Godoy and Maria Louisa. You will be banished, your lands and your estate will be confiscated. . . ."

"Your Majesty!" Don Diego gasped, his face contorted with anguish.

Charles IV held up a placating hand and forced a wan smile to his trembling lips. "Hear me out, Don Diego. I know your worth to our nation. You are herewith appointed intendant in the province of Taos, in Nuevo Mexico."

Don Diego de Escobar uttered a choking groan. To be banished forever from his beloved Madrid—it was like a sentence of death. And to uproot his family, with his wife already grievously ill, and move to a desolate country in the New World appeared to be an irretrievable disaster.

But Charles IV had risen and approached Don Diego. He placed his hand on the latter's shoulder. "Come, my old friend, it is not so bad. Believe me, I argued earnestly against the wishes of Godoy and my queen. It was only by such argument that I prevailed in being able to grant you five thousand acres of good land and this position of intendant. It will bring you five thousand pesos in annual salary. I know you will find other benefits. I am quite certain of it, indeed." Again the king smiled wanly.

"I do not know what to say, my king. . . ."

The king patted Don Diego's shoulder. "Take heart from what I have been able to do for you. Do you not see that, in the broader sense, I agree with you that we must maintain our distant empire? I understand your wish to keep Spain great among the nations of the world. It is my wish, too—you know that. And it is my belief that you are best suited to this new station in life. You will be free of the intrigues of court. Ah yes . . ." Charles IV sighed and shook his head. "I know, far better than you, the wearisome pomp and formalities which surround me on every side."

Don Diego drew his sword and tendered it to his king, as a token of his resignation of all stature. But Charles IV shook his head and gently grasped the nobleman's wrist as he forced him to sheathe the blade. "No, you must not. You must, instead, look upon this new post as a reward for your valued labors. I, whom you call your king and to whom you have pledged your devotion, believe in and rely on you. You must think that always."

There were tears in Don Diego's eyes as he slowly knelt and kissed the king's hand. Once again, he swore allegiance, just as his father had done before him in the presence of Charles III.

"My majordomo has already received the documents you will give the governor of Cuba and, as well, a letter of introduction to our viceroy in Mexico. From there, you will be given a military escort to your new post in Taos."

This news, far from cheering Don Diego, only distressed him more. It would be an arduous journey for his sick wife and young children.

As if to emphasize the disaster even more, Charles IV spoke again, in a firmer, more decisive tone. "The galleon *Paloma* will carry you and your family on the journey, Don Diego. I should be grateful to you if you could arrange to depart no later than the end of this month. The *Paloma* is now being outfitted for the voyage."

"I hear and I obey, my king." Once again, Don Diego knelt and, bowing his head, kissed the hand of his royal master. Then, his face impassive, striving to control the emotions which welled up within him, he left the antechamber.

As he closed the door behind him, he stopped short and his eyes narrowed with a sudden, rising anger. There before him, chatting convivially with the major-domo, was the Count Jorge de Murciano. Don Diego's hand gripped the hilt of his sword, seized by the impulse to denounce the scheming rogue and to challenge him to a duel. Yet, mastering himself with the greatest effort, he straightened his shoulders and walked forward proudly.

"Oh, Don Diego de Escobar, what a happy and fortuitous meeting!" Count Jorge de Murciano approached the gray-haired nobleman and extended his hand in greeting.

"If you say so, Count de Murciano," Don Diego retorted. "If you will excuse me, my wife is ill and I must return home at once. To you, majordomo, my sincere thanks. And you, Count, I have the pleasure of wishing you a very good morning."

Without looking back, ignoring the soft, mocking laugh that he heard behind him, Don Diego de Escobar walked slowly out of the Escorial.

Now alone, John Cooper must brave the wilderness in his trek west. After a number of unexpected adventures he meets up with the Escobars who have found their way to Taos. John's life becomes passionately entwined with the family.

(Read the complete Bantam Book, available June 1st wherever paperbacks are sold.)